"Shh. You'll wake the neighbors."

"Serves you right. I hope they call the police," Chelsea said, her laugh muffled against Nick's chest.

She gripped his tie as she righted herself and, too late, heard him make a choking sound. "I'm sorry, Nick," she apologized.

"You're going to be the death of me yet."

"Well, who in their right mind wears a tie at this time of night anyway?" She turned to face him, reaching for the knot. "Mind if I at least loosen it?" Her eyes lifted to his and what she saw made her heart slam against her ribs.

"Be my guest," he answered huskily. "I haven't been undressed by a woman in at least . . . well, too long."

Shannon Waverly lives in Massachusetts with her husband, a high school English teacher. Their two children are both in college. Shannon wrote her first romance at the age of twelve, and she's been writing ever since. She says that in her first year of college, she joined the literary magazine and ''promptly submitted the most pompous allegory imaginable. The editor at the time just as promptly rejected it. But he also asked me out. He and I have now been married for over twenty-one years.''

Books by Shannon Waverly

HARLEQUIN ROMANCE
3072—A SUMMER KIND OF LOVE
3150—NO TRESPASSING

NEW LEASE ON LOVE

Shannon Waverly

Harlequin Books

TORONTO • NEW YORK • LONDON
AMSTERDAM • PARIS • SYDNEY • HAMBURG
STOCKHOLM • ATHENS • TOKYO • MILAN
MADRID • WARSAW • BUDAPEST • AUCKLAND

My deepest thanks to Dave Gifford of
Balloon Adventures of New Bedford, Inc.

Author's note:
If any deviations from accepted ballooning
practices appear in this book,
they are inadvertent and mine alone.

ISBN 0-373-03204-8

Harlequin Romance first edition June 1992

NEW LEASE ON LOVE

CHAPTER ONE

"THIS ISN'T MY LEASE!" Chelsea dropped the crisp stationery on the kitchen table and frowned. April was the month she always renewed it, but she was used to signing for a whole year. This thing was only good for a month!

She sat back, rereading the note Mr. Lockwood had included, but all it told her was that the Pine Ridge ski area, which he owned and on whose fringe her house sat, was in a temporary state of flux. "Don't be concerned," he'd added in his familiar broad scrawl. "Go about business as usual. Matters should stabilize soon."

Chelsea's bewilderment deepened into anxiety. Not that Mr. Lockwood had given her any indication that she should be worried, but something was going on up the road at Pine Ridge, and she wished she knew what it was.

She walked to the sink and poured her suddenly unappetizing coffee down the drain. Outside, a mixture of rain and snow, driven by a cold, gray wind, was pelting the greening lawn and confusing the daffodils. Winter died hard here in the mountains of western Massachusetts.

Chelsea had canceled this morning's charter because of the unseasonable weather. But then, hot-air balloon flights had to be cancelled for reasons far less serious than a late-April sleet. Ballooning was a thin, precarious business, and lately she'd been wondering how much longer she could stick it out. She earned a marginal living at best, and at the age of twenty-six this was beginning to depress her. She didn't want to be wealthy. All she'd ever wanted was to be self-sufficient. But the truth was, if she hadn't worked at other jobs along the way to supplement her income, Balloon the Berkshires would have folded years ago.

Living anywhere else would've scuttled her business, too, she thought with growing concern. The rent she'd paid Mr. Lockwood these last six years was inordinately low, especially in light of what she got for her money. Her house was quite large, nine rooms, one of which she'd converted to an office, and it had an attached barn that was perfect for storing her ballooning equipment and doing repairs. Her lease also gave her permission to launch her balloon from a meadow up the road and to maintain a billboard along its edge.

Chelsea especially appreciated that meadow. Not only was it close to home and office, it was also strategically located along the busy road to Pine Ridge. Skiers driving by couldn't possibly miss her billboard, and most of the time the breeze took her balloon right over the slopes and their curious upturned eyes.

Chelsea knew she'd never find a setup better suited to her purposes, but even with low rent, finances were often tight, and on a bleak day like today, it was easy to start thinking she'd reached a crossroads in her life. Perhaps it was time to stop dreaming she could make a living from ballooning and to start training for something real.

The only problem was, she loved what she was doing now. Since the age of twelve, when her grandfather and all his gear had moved in with her family, she'd never wanted to work at anything else.

The wall clock chimed, reminding her that Mimi, her brother Larry's wife, had called from work earlier, looking for a ride home. Her car was being repaired, and Larry had a faculty meeting after school and couldn't stop by for her. It was now three-thirty. Mimi's shift at the hospital was almost done.

Chelsea picked up the lease and, as she headed for the front hall, skimmed it again, but another reading left her no more enlightened. She leaned into her office and tossed the document onto her desk. From the opposite wall, a bright, framed poster of a balloon in flight proclaimed: "Life's too short not to take the adventure!" Some adventure, Chelsea thought, glancing at the stack of bills her lease had landed on.

She opened the hall closet and surveyed the contents, looking for the proper battle gear for today's weather. From the hospital, she and Mimi would have to run by the sitter's to pick up nine-month-old Beth. After that, they'd retrieve Mimi's two boys from their friend's, where the school bus dropped them off on the three afternoons their mother worked.

Chelsea shook her head as she pulled her green vinyl rain poncho off its hanger. Two people who were as active as Larry and Mimi had no business trying to raise three children. It was a wonder they weren't all neurotic.

Actually they were thriving, kids and parents alike, and quite often Chelsea found herself envying them. Not that she was ready to settle down just yet herself. Too much energy still had to be channeled into her business. She wanted Balloon the Berkshires to be firmly established and prospering before she got seriously involved with anyone. Entering a relationship as an independent, self-sufficient person was important to her. Her mother had never worked outside the home—until she was widowed—and the transition had been traumatic.

The way things were going, though, Chelsea figured she wouldn't be able to settle down until she was ninety-two. It seemed that every penny she'd ever earned had gone back into her business—into purchasing equipment, furnishing this office and converting the barn out back to a work space.

Then there was always advertising and insurance and repairs...

She'd thought this would be a pivotal year, the year when
her investments would start to reap a noticeable profit. Last
year had been so promising she'd even quit cashiering at the
market. Now she didn't see it happening. The weather had
been abominable, the economy even worse.

The arrival of this new one-month lease wasn't helping
matters any, either. It just underscored the precariousness
of her situation, because the reality was that she didn't own
this house where she'd lived and conducted business for the
last six years. She didn't own the barn out back where she
stored and repaired her equipment. And she didn't own the
meadow where she advertised and launched her flights. All
the underpinnings of her life were rented and therefore
controlled by someone else.

She and Mr. Lockwood had enjoyed a pleasant relationship until now, one that was mutually beneficial. He had no
use for her house or meadow, while to her they were absolutely vital. She only hoped her apprehensions were un-
founded and their relationship wasn't about to change. She
didn't know how she'd swing a higher rent, if that was what
was on his mind, and she strongly suspected it was. She'd
have to go back to cashiering—and probably take in house-
mates, besides—not a scenario she relished. Ah, well, she'd
just have to adjust, she supposed. Ever since her kid sister,
Judy, had married and moved out, the house had been too
quiet, anyway.

Chelsea rummaged in the wardrobe for boots, hating the
thought of the inch of slush already blanketing the ground.
All she came up with, though, were the puffy maroon things
that matched the down coat she'd already given away. Her
brother considered her the family's free spirit of fashion.
Still, when she glanced at her reflection, even she had to
groan. The poncho made her look like a three-masted

schooner at full sail, and those boots resembled tree stumps! She hadn't put on any makeup today, either, and because of the weather, her short bob was curling defiantly. With a disgusted huff, she tugged up her hood and headed for the door.

The hospital was a few miles down the valley on the outskirts of the village. Chelsea pulled her Jeep into the lot at the rear of the building, found a parking spot, then dashed out into the elements, head ducked against the angled sleet. Slush splashed into her boots. "Dang!" she swore, shivering. She hopped a puddle at the curb, landed with an off-balance, one-footed slide and continued up the walk at a run.

At the top of the steps she threw her shoulder against the heavy glass door. "Excuse me, I'm so sorry," she apologized as she collided with someone in the muddy entranceway. She shook out her hair, wet curls sticking to her cheek and forehead.

"No problem."

She raised her eyes, drawn by a warm, deep voice. The man she'd bumped into wasn't wearing a coat. Probably just taking a break from visiting a patient, she surmised. She smiled, hoping to convey her apology again.

She stamped her feet to knock the slush off them, then searched her shoulder bag for a tissue to dry her face. "Crazy New England weather," she felt compelled to say, sharing the small entranceway with him as she was. "Can't decide if it's winter or spring."

"They say it's the cruelest month, April." He spoke in that friendly way strangers adopt when momentarily sharing a shelter on a stormy day.

"I remember that. Chaucer, right?"

He smiled and shrugged. "Somebody."

Chelsea got the feeling he knew exactly who, and it wasn't Chaucer. Even as she was searching her memory, though, he returned to watching the storm, bringing the conversation to an end.

She tossed the tissue into a disposal bin and gave the man another sidelong peek. He had a disarming sort of handsomeness about him, the sort that took a person totally by surprise and left her slightly dizzy. He was muscularly lean and tall, six feet or more, with thick nut-brown hair and deep hazel eyes that glinted with flecks of gold. He had a straight classic nose, a firm sensually drawn mouth and a well-defined slightly cleft chin.

But it wasn't so much his physical features that struck Chelsea as handsome, though they were uncommonly so. It was...well, she really couldn't put her finger on what was so striking about this man. All she knew was that she'd never felt another person's...presence so intensely before.

She swallowed with an uncomfortable dry gulp, realizing that she was staring. Not that he'd noticed. He seemed to have withdrawn into himself, reeled in whatever lines of communication the situation had drawn out of him. Feeling unaccountably disappointed, she left him to his musing and pushed her way through the inner door.

The receptionist put down her phone. "Hey, Chelsea! What are you doing here today?"

"Hi, Carol. Just picking up Mimi. She still working?"

"Uh-huh. Want to go in?" The receptionist gestured toward the corridor behind her marked Physical Therapy.

"No. I'll take a seat and wait."

Chelsea found the only available seat in the crowded waiting alcove. The one next to it was vacant, too, but someone had already claimed it with a dark gray topcoat. A blend of cashmere and wool, she guessed. Well made, attractive and expensive.

She unzipped her green poncho and let it fall aside, revealing black tights above the maroon boots, a straight black skirt, and a chunky yellow sweater. She had to admit she was almost as colorful today as one of her balloons. She reached for a *Good Housekeeping* magazine and opened it at random.

"Excuse me," a familiar voice murmured.

Chelsea glanced up and found the stranger she'd barreled into staring at her outstretched legs. "Oh, sorry." As she tucked her feet beneath her chair, her cheeks warmed. Which was absurd, she reminded herself. Blocking someone's path wasn't that grievous a faux pas. Or was it rather because that someone was the man from the entranceway and he was settling into the seat beside her?

Chelsea screwed her attention back on the magazine but soon realized she wasn't absorbing a word she read. For some reason, her mind kept returning to the man beside her, like a radio determined to pick up only one station clearly.

She took a stealthy peep sideways. He was reading, too— *Business Weekly*. How odd, she thought, the protocol of people in waiting rooms. Although they had spoken just minutes before, there was no social law that mandated they now acknowledge that meeting. They were just strangers, isolated within whatever private reasons had brought them here. She wished that fact didn't bother her so much.

Unwittingly, Chelsea let out a sigh, and though he didn't even blink, she felt his attention shift from his magazine to her. A strange, uncomfortable heat rose through her body, pulsing from her skin, until she thought her vinyl poncho would melt.

What was wrong with her, anyway? It wasn't as if she was starved for male companionship. She dated. All the time. No one in particular, of course, but that shouldn't matter.

Chelsea sat tight, trying to conjure up the image of the handsomest male friend she had, but all she could think of was the man sitting next to her. The magazine print swam out of focus as she watched him cross his leg, ankle over knee, as she caught a faint scent of warm wool and a lime-scented after-shave...

In spite of her discomfort, she began to smile. A few years earlier, she and Mimi had bought a dog-eared copy of *Fear of Flying* at a yard sale. After they'd both read it—at lightning speed, she remembered—they'd had a hilarious discussion about the idea at the heart of the controversial novel, namely that a woman could fantasize as wildly about meaningless sex as any man, that she could be on a bus and spot a stranger across the aisle and...

The man beside her uncrossed his legs and shifted his weight as if he was finding the chair suddenly uncomfortable.

When they'd read *Fear of Flying,* Mimi was already married to Chelsea's brother and the mother of two boys. Yet, even she had admitted to a few R-rated daydreams involving Tom Selleck, and at the time, Chelsea had been quite taken with Christopher Reeve. But neither of them had been adventurous enough to sketch out scenarios featuring the spontaneous, uninvolved sex suggested in the book. Both were too hopelessly romantic. Violins and moonbeams usually intruded somewhere in the fantasies.

Well, then, had either of them ever passed a stranger on the street, or shared a bus or plane with someone she'd found instantly appealing? A ship passing in the night who would haunt her memory forever?

Mimi said she had. "But I married him as fast as I could," she'd added with a laugh.

Chelsea had felt vaguely cheated. She'd never enjoyed such an experience herself. She'd dated, she'd felt affection for several acquaintances, perhaps even a measure of love for a few. But she'd never met anyone who'd had that instantly distracting effect on her, that riveting aura and ability to "rattle her teeth" with just a glance, as Mimi phrased it.

Not until today.

From the corner of her eye, she studied his hands clasping the magazine. Strong, clean, capable hands, with long fingers and bony knuckles. Hands that wore no ring, she noticed. Now *that* was unusual. Men like him were almost always taken. Maybe he was divorced?

She liked the way he dressed, too, which came as no little surprise. Usually she didn't go for the buttoned-down, polished-shoe type, but he carried the look well. The crisp white shirt and maroon tie showing over his ribbed black sweater indicated a vein of restraint in his personality, and his tailored charcoal pants did nothing to relax the image. Nevertheless, she liked the clothes—on him—and she loved the sweater. It was earthy, casual—but hardly careless. No, carelessness was the least part of this man's character. He was thoroughly deliberate, deliberate in the way he tied his shoes, combed his hair to one side, folded the cuffs of his sweater...

He turned, slowly, and looked right into Chelsea's eyes, one of his brows arched in a silent question. He didn't look amused.

Chelsea's gaze zoomed back to her magazine, her heart hammering. With one stern glance he'd made her realize how absurd the last ten minutes had been. Fantasy and imagination were fine in their place, but this was not one of those places. Her mind had wandered inappropriately, and what was worse, he somehow knew it.

She rose from her chair. "I've d-decided to go meet Mimi after all," she stammered to the receptionist on her way by.

The wing where her sister-in-law worked was filled with a mystifying assortment of exercise equipment. When Chelsea spotted her, Mimi was leaning over a little girl on a machine that somewhat resembled a bicycle.

"Chelsea! Hi!" Mimi smiled her patentedly warm nurse-smile. "Five more minutes, okay?"

"Don't rush."

Mimi, freckle-faced and red-haired, leaned over to adjust a tension monitor.

The child looked up at her gloomily. "Can I stop now?"

"Almost done, Katie. You're doing super." Mimi motioned for an attendant to take her place before walking over.

"New patient?" Chelsea asked.

"Hm. Brand new." Mimi's lips tightened.

"She sure is cute."

"If you ignore her fascination with four-letter words and a bite to shame a rottweiler."

"Her? She looks like Shirley Temple, for heaven's sake! She can't be any older than six or seven."

Mimi nodded indignantly. "That's right. Seven." Slowly her smile returned, easing out the scowl, and when she murmured, "Poor lamb," her voice was soft with compassion.

Chelsea watched the little girl struggling to press the pedals of her machine, her small full mouth pursed in a pout, her blond curls bouncing around her dimpled face—and mutiny simmering in her blue eyes.

"What's her problem? Anything serious?"

"Not anymore. Her right leg was injured in an accident three years ago. She's had several operations to correct the damage, but she's still left with thin muscles that need strengthening, and a limp, which may or may not disappear with time, we aren't certain."

"Any more surgery down the road?"

Mimi shook her head. "Just therapy. But she's been through so much already I'm afraid she's had her fill of hospitals. She wants no part of doctors or nurses or..." She paused and a light went on behind her eyes. "Say..."

Chelsea's gaze skittered around the room, searching for an exit. She recognized that look. "Mimi, you know I've taken on too many kids as it is. I'm barely making any money now.''

''But she's so tiny. You could slip her in with a group of paying passengers, and nobody'd even notice.''

''I'll have to think about it.''

''Look at her, Chelsea.''

Purposely, Chelsea did not look. She knew she'd be a dead duck if she did. ''I said I'll think about it.''

''Please do. I have a feeling she's the type who'd really benefit from your attention.''

Chelsea had been taking children from the hospital up in her balloon for years. The idea occurred to her after a couple chartered a flight to celebrate their son's eighth birthday. Only after the child died four weeks later did Chelsea learn that he had had cancer. His parents, who were fairly well-off, had let him make up a ''wish list,'' and taking a balloon ride was the thing he wanted to do most. After his death they'd called to thank Chelsea again. Their son, they said, had talked about his ride right up to the end.

Chelsea had felt gratified, knowing she'd created a moment of happiness for the boy, but she'd also felt shaken and angry because of his death. She'd called Mimi, hoping some of her professional objectivity would rub off, but Mimi was no help that night. If anything, she'd made Chelsea feel worse, opening her eyes to the numbers of children in the area who were seriously ill, children whose parents, for the most part, couldn't afford the luxury of granting dying wishes.

Chelsea had lain awake that night, the cogs of her mind whirring away. If an hour's balloon ride had meant so much to one sick child, maybe it would mean something to others. The next morning she'd called Mimi again and with her help began to make connections at the hospital.

At first Chelsea gave rides only to seriously ill children, for no other reason than to get their minds off their situation. Then she came up with the idea of using rides as a reward for the children enduring chemotherapy or other painful treatments. Finally, unable to exclude anyone, she'd extended her rides to the children's ward in general. She found her program worked especially well with the kids in physical therapy. That promise of a balloon ride really motivated them to exercise hard. She even had a system of "tickets" that they earned at therapy and presented to her the day of their flight.

"Is her mother here?" Chelsea asked. "You know I'll have to talk to her first."

"Uh, no. According to Katie's records, her mother is deceased."

"Oh, that poor—"

"Hey, does that mean you're taking Katie on?"

Chelsea sighed, disgusted with her lack of backbone. "Looks like."

"Great." Mimi took Chelsea by the arm. "Come on. I'll introduce you to her father."

Something shot through Chelsea at that moment, a jet of improbable anticipation. Waiting by the reception desk, she held her breath while Mimi ventured into the sitting area. When Mimi touched the arm of the man she'd bumped into earlier, her sense of anticipation exploded into a million arrows of fire.

Mimi's words hit with a delayed reaction: Katie's mother was deceased—which meant this man was a widower. Chelsea tried to feel sorry for his loss, but all her emotions seemed momentarily occupied with the knowledge that he was single.

Chelsea watched his lean body tense. He asked if his daughter was all right, then jumped to his feet, apparently still not convinced that she was, and followed Mimi to the reception station. Puzzlement compounded worry when he saw Chelsea waiting there.

"Are you sure Katie's okay?" he asked again.

"She's doing great, Mr. Tanner. I'm sorry if I alarmed you," Mimi went on soothingly. "I merely wanted to introduce you to someone, my sister-in-law, Chelsea Lawton."

The lines between his eyes deepened as his assessing gaze swept over Chelsea. After the way she'd been checking him out earlier, he probably thought she'd arranged this introduction. Embarrassment warmed her cheeks until she was sure they were glowing bright pink.

"Hi," he ventured warily, extending his hand. "I'm Nick Tanner."

She shook his hand. It conveyed a sense warmth and solid strength the way no handshake ever had before.

"Well, I should be getting back to Katie," Mimi interjected. "See you in a few minutes."

Nick Tanner watched Mimi's retreating figure as if trying to figure out a puzzle, then he turned that perplexed gaze on Chelsea.

"What's this all about?" he asked guardedly.

With his undivided attention on her, Chelsea found it hard to breathe. *Concentrate, you idiot!* she reprimanded herself sharply. *Stop imagining this man sailing off into the sunset with you in your balloon.*

She cleared her throat. "Mr. Tanner," she began.

"Miss Lawton," he replied with a hint of amusement. One eyebrow cocked as his glittering hazel eyes traveled from her hair, which she imagined was an unruly mop by now, down her unlikely-green poncho, to her maroon boots.

She cleared her throat again. "I run a business called Balloon the Berkshires..."

His expression changed at the edges, subtly, like a quick flash of heat lightning in summer. "Balloon...?"

"Yes. Manned. I'm the owner of a hot-air balloon business. People charter flights with me, I give lessons, do promotions. Occasionally I...I also take up children who are patients here." She wet her lips nervously. His eyes were narrowing, a coolness straightening his spine.

"Go on," he said.

Chelsea had liked his voice before, but those two short words positively frosted the air. She blinked in confusion. What was happening here? What was she doing wrong? Usually, people became fascinated when she told them what she did for a living.

"We've f-found that most children really love the experience of ballooning, and it can often be used as leverage during the course of their therapy."

"I don't understand." As if to punctuate the point, he folded his arms across his black sweater.

Summoning all her courage, she continued, "We don't like using the word 'bribe,' but, in essence, that's what it is. The promise of a balloon ride helps get young patients through boring or painful therapy."

"We? Who's we?" he said in a sudden burst of irritation. "Are you affiliated with this hospital?"

She gulped. "No. But I'm in close touch with each child's doctor and—"

"And obviously you've taken a notion to foist Katie into your...your balloon program." He was visibly upset now, his voice grating with sarcasm.

"Mimi, the nurse who introduced us...she thinks Katie's the sort of case who'd really benefit—"

"Case! You make my daughter sound like a guinea pig in some damn experiment." The receptionist looked over, embarrassed for Chelsea.

"I'm sorry. I phrased that poorly. I certainly didn't mean—"

"And I'd really prefer my daughter didn't learn to make her way through life on bribes."

"Rewards, Mr. Tanner. Think of them as rewards." Chelsea ran an unsteady hand across her forehead. She'd never received a reaction like this from a parent before. Usually they were thankful and appreciative of her efforts.

"Sometimes," she stumbled on, "these kids have been through so much they've lost patience with their treatment. They lose hope, even their sense of joy. Occasionally, ballooning can help them get it back."

He listened, his eyes running over her with disconcerting thoroughness. Then, "I'm not interested, Miss Lawton." He started to move away.

Impulsively, Chelsea clutched his arm. He tensed and looked at her hand in disdain. She pulled it back, growing hot with humiliation. "Sorry. I've explained myself quite badly, I'm afraid. The first thing I should've told you is that I don't charge for these rides. They're free."

"That hardly affects my decision. I can afford your rides, and I still don't want Katie up in one of those damn things." People in the waiting room were staring at them now.

"One of those *damn* things?" she repeated incredulously. "Mr. Tanner, hot-air balloons are perfectly safe, and I'm a fully qualified, licensed pilot."

"Excuse me. I'm just not interested," he said, brushing past her.

"I'm sorry."

He stopped. "Sorry? That seems to be a popular word in your vocabulary. And what would you do if you got into an accident with one of these kids? Say you're sorry?"

"An accident? I don't have accidents, Mr. Tanner," she bit out crisply. "You obviously don't understand."

"I understand perfectly. Do you?" His stare was daunting.

Her shoulders slumped. "I understand." She could cross Katie's name off her passenger list. But she knew she was disappointed on a deeper level. Absurdly, she regretted having lost the opportunity to get to know this man better.

No, she amended. Not *this* man, but the fantasy she'd concocted. Apparently, the two were not the same.

"Well, let me give you my card, in case you change your mind," she said. "I can be reached at my office on Pine Ridge Road. The phone number's there."

Nick Tanner's dark head swung up, an odd stillness in his eyes. "Of course."

"What? Are you familiar with my business?"

The silence spun out as he stared at her, and for once, he seemed the one who was feeling uneasy.

"Something wrong, Mr. Tanner?"

He rubbed a hand over his face and sighed. "Well, I guess we were bound to meet eventually, anyway."

The afternoon was quickly taking on a surreal quality. "I don't understand."

"I've just bought into the Pine Ridge ski area up the road from you. I'm Chet Lockwood's new business partner and, I suppose, your new landlord."

Chelsea's trembling started at her scalp and ended with her toes. Nick Tanner was the mysterious "state of flux" at Pine Ridge? She was too stunned to say anything and fortunately didn't have to, because at that moment Katie came bounding down the corridor.

"All done, Daddy," she announced.

Nick seemed to forget Chelsea immediately. Smiling, he held out his arms, and his daughter leapt into them.

"Now let's go," the child said adamantly.

He squeezed her tight and kissed her blond curls. "Anything you say, boss." He set her down, took her coat from Mimi and carefully slipped it on her.

"Let's *go!*"

"Wait a sec, Spud. We've got to button up first."

As shaken as Chelsea was, there was no missing the love that burned in his eyes.

"See you next week, Katie," Mimi called, but the child refused to turn around. She undoubtedly had no intention of returning to this hospital.

With feelings too muddled to understand anymore, Chelsea watched father and daughter leave. In spite of her pronounced limp, Katie carried herself as aloof as a queen, defiant as a devil. Chelsea also noticed she was clinging to her father's hand as if it was a lifeline.

CHAPTER TWO

"WHAT A MORNING, Kate! Isn't it terrific?" Nick stood on the front steps of the Lockwood home, took a deep breath and expelled it with a slow, satisfied "ahhh."

Behind him, Katie yawned and rubbed her eyes. "Why can't I stay here?"

His shoulders sagged. He'd thought they were done arguing. "I already told you, Grace can't watch you today. She has to go to a wedding with her father."

"I can stay alone."

"Oh, no, you can't." Nick knew what his daughter was up to. She wanted to sit in front of the TV and watch cartoons. Since moving into this house ten days ago, Katie had been doing a lot of that. Nick hadn't been aware so many cartoon shows even existed, and he was beginning to think that Grace, in a misguided effort to please Katie, was helping her search them out. That was the main reason he wanted her to come along today. Besides, the weather was too nice to waste indoors. That sleet a couple of days ago had been winter's last gasp. The temperature was now a balmy seventy degrees, even at seven in the morning, and flowers and leaves were bursting out everywhere.

"I thought you were looking forward to going to work with me, Spud."

"I am, I am." Katie didn't sound very eager, though.

Nick sympathized. It was early and it was Saturday. But his new computer had arrived, and twenty years of jumbled financial data needed to be sorted and entered. The job was formidable, and Nick wondered again how Pine Ridge had managed to stay open so long. Chet Lockwood had no business sense at all. Fortunately, he knew skiing, knew the sport better than anyone Nick had ever met. Together they'd make a good team.

"Got your toys?" he asked.

"Yup." Katie nudged her canvas bag with a sneakered foot.

Nick made a thumbs-up gesture before opening the car door for her. Besides the storybooks, crayons and Legos that usually kept her entertained, he'd made sure to include a jump rope and a ball. She'd spent too much of her young life in hospital beds and plaster casts. She needed to get out in the sunshine and exercise. Any movement would do, and if it was fun, all the better.

As he was about to drive off, the front door opened, and Grace Lockwood waved to get his attention. She was still in her bathrobe, the long pink quilted thing with the large pearl buttons that looked like the one his mother used to wear.

"Nickie!" she called. He rolled down the car window. "What would you like for dinner tonight?"

Nick rubbed his hand over his clean-shaven jaw and thought. Dinner. He wasn't used to thinking about dinner with the taste of orange juice still on his tongue. Fresh-squeezed orange juice, at that.

"I don't care. Anything."

"Oh, come on, give me some help. Pot roast? Chicken? I make a nice Chicken Kiev."

Nick rubbed his jaw again. Every evening so far, she'd prepared them a great dinner. Having kept house for her father since her mother died five years ago, Grace was one terrific cook. But sometimes her meals were a bit too exotic for Katie's palate. He hated to admit it, but the formality of her dining room was beginning to wear on him, too. Besides, preparing these elaborate meals took so much time.

"How about if we go out to eat, Grace? After being at a wedding all day, I'm sure you won't feel like cooking."

"I don't mind." She patted her smooth page boy, which looked remarkably the same now as it had last night.

"But even Julia Child must step out once in a while."

She giggled. "Oh, all right. If you insist."

Nick waved, threw the car into gear and set off down the quiet street of the quiet Berkshire town. Beside him, securely strapped into her seat, Katie sighed with relief and said, "Thanks, Dad. And let's make it McDonald's, okay?"

Nick threw back his head and laughed. "What's the matter? Don't you like Grace's cooking?"

Katie averted her gaze out the side window. "When are we gonna get our own house?"

"Soon, baby. Soon. I'm going to look at a few apartments this week." Nick drove on, past the other dignified colonial homes that rimmed the village green, by the graceful white church with its five-tiered spire catching the early sun.

He knew Grace was doing her best to please his daughter, but for some reason, Katie refused to warm to her, and he wondered what her reaction would be if he told her he was thinking of marrying Grace.

Of course, Katie realized he and Grace were dating, but he didn't think she suspected he was considering marriage. Why should she? He'd dated other women and hadn't married them. Just a couple of women, actually. But then, Laura had been dead for only three years.

Laura. He'd been thinking about her a lot these past few days. It had been a surprisingly long time since he had, too. What surprised him even more was finding his pain and sorrow nearly gone. Only the emptiness remained. And the anger, of course. But he suspected that would never completely go away.

Oddly, it was that girl with the hot-air balloon business who'd triggered this current rash of memories. Chelsea Lawton.

Chelsea. Nice name. Different, like her. She'd caught his eye as soon as she'd dashed out of her Jeep, that bright green poncho flapping in the wind, the determined way she'd fought the sleet . . .

Nick really couldn't say why she reminded him of Laura. Physically, they were completely different. Laura's hair had been long and blond, while Chelsea's was short, springy, and so dark a brown it was nearly black. Laura had been tall and willow-slender, whereas Chelsea barely cleared his chin, and every inch of her was soft and curved. There was no earthly reason for him to connect the two, but he did nonetheless.

Maybe it had something to do with the uneasiness he'd been feeling since meeting her, the uncertainty, as if the ground beneath his feet had suddenly begun to pitch and roll—which, of course, was completely intolerable. He'd worked too hard these past three years to take rational control of his life, sweating over choices, eliminating anything that threatened his well-being or Katie's.

But every time he thought of Chelsea Lawton, his carefully ordered life seemed about to be upended. She projected a raw energy, a vitality—a something—that made him feel oddly vulnerable. Perhaps that was the connection.

With ten years' worth of hindsight, Nick realized he never should've married Laura, but at twenty-two, he'd been too young and lovestruck to know any better. True, his love for her had probably been the force that had propelled his amazing bank career. And true, he'd been happier with her than he'd ever been before.

But he'd also been miserable. As time had pulled the veil from his eyes, he'd watched the very qualities that had attracted him to her sharpen and distort. Her adventurous spirit, her spontaneity and independence—he finally saw them for what they really were, nothing more than ego-centrism, immaturity and recklessness.

Not even Katie's birth had changed her life-style. He'd thought it would. Not that he'd wanted to put Laura in a cage or anything, but did she have to enter *all* those motor-cycle races? Did she have to drive so fast *all* the time, even to the corner store? And did she have to take Katie with her?

Nick's hands whitened around the steering wheel. Laura almost *had* taken Katie with her. When he'd seen his tiny daughter's broken body splayed out on the emergency-room table, he'd thought for sure he'd lose her, too.

Without a doubt, that was the worst day of his life. He remembered it with perfect clarity—the timbre of the po-liceman's voice calling him at work...the words "There's been an accident"...the sense that his nightmare, the nameless terror he'd been living with since falling in love with Laura, had finally taken solid form.

He'd left a client sitting at his desk and raced across town, his driving so erratic it was a wonder he hadn't had an ac-cident himself. Then the blinding hospital lights...and dreamlike words falling from a policeman's mouth, words clanging like steeple bells in his brain...

They'd shown him Laura's body, but she'd looked too beautiful. She'd looked as if she were just sleeping, and Nick had tried to rouse her. She refused to awaken, though, no matter how hard he'd tried, and the doctor's words about a broken neck finally joined the rest of the clanging in his overheated brain. That was when the rage had struck, tear-ing through him like a runaway train.

Unfortunately, the doctor chose that very moment to tell him about Katie, that she'd been on the bike, too. Nick re-membered grabbing him and shoving him hard against a wall. Luckily, the police were there to restrain him and help make him realize Katie was still alive.

Katie. He'd been appalled by how banged up she was. He'd never felt such pain in his life. Even now, he could see her—her eyes begging him to save her, reproaching him for having let this awful thing happen. That look would remain with him forever.

He would never forgive Laura for causing Katie to suffer so, but Laura wasn't the only person Nick blamed. He couldn't help thinking he was at fault, too. He could have tried harder to change her, to deter her, or at least to protect Katie. Granted, he had argued with Laura. Toward the end, they seemed to do nothing else. But was it enough? Couldn't he have found some other way to get through to her? Weren't there measures he could have taken to ensure Katie's safety?

But he hadn't. He'd failed to stop Laura. He'd failed—and for this he'd feel responsible the rest of his days.

Katie's plight had forced Nick to pull himself together immediately. Laura might be gone, but Katie was still alive, and she needed him. For the next two weeks, except for the funeral, he never left her side. Sitting there watching her, there were times when he felt that his strength was her strength, and if he gave up, so would she. *He* was keeping her alive by sheer willpower and vigilance.

Katie's doctors eventually took her name off the critical list, and after weeks of being strong for Katie, Nick collapsed in exhaustion. It was then, lying in his own bed at home, that he realized he was alone, and that he would be forever. Laura was never coming back. Until then, the reality hadn't sunk in.

Months passed in a blur of sorrow. He returned to work, he paid the bills, he bought groceries. He functioned. But Nick remembered it only as a time of putting one foot in front of the other, and he often wondered if he would've done even that if it hadn't been for Katie. Because of her, he kept going. He had to be strong, through her painful recovery, through repeated surgery.

Nights, however, remained difficult for the better part of a year. With most of his energy sapped during the day, he often dropped at night into a morass of loneliness and wanting Laura back. And rage. Rage was always there, too, wound through his pain, deep and tight. He'd curse Laura's self-centeredness and stupidity. She'd had no right doing this to him and Katie. But when the cursing was done, he'd turn to the cold half of the bed and fall asleep clutching her pillow. That, he discovered, was the dark side of love; the deeper it ran, the sharper was the anguish.

There was nothing he could do about all that love now. It had already been given. But he could certainly guard against the future.

Friends had tried to tell him otherwise. They'd introduced him to women, encouraged him to give love another chance. One day even Katie's doctor had talked to him about "getting back in the swing." And he'd obliged them—on the surface. He'd taken women out, to dinner, to concerts and the theater. But none of those well-meaning friends or experts had been through what he'd suffered. They hadn't a clue.

No, there would be no more loving in his life. No dizzy raptures. No blind leaps into marriage. He was an adult now, not a raw kid. From here on in, he'd be in control. Love might have its highs, but it also had its lows. And Nick didn't need any more tickets to the dark side of the moon.

That was what he found so appealing about Grace. He saw her without the distortion that came with high emotion, and what he saw convinced him she'd be good for him and Katie. She was everything Laura hadn't been. She loved to tend house, to cook and clean and fuss over the people in her life. And she was responsible. Even the thought of Grace Lockwood riding a motorcycle was ludicrous.

Of course, they'd probably never know the kind of physical excitement he'd shared with Laura, but he was well past the point of believing sexual attraction was the basis of a good, lasting marriage. He and Laura had shared a fiery attraction, yet the rest of their marriage had been in shambles. Grace had so much more to offer: stability, a reassuringly calm life-style—and chocolate-chip cookies fresh from the oven at least once a week. Katie desperately needed someone like Grace in her life, and one of these days he should get off the fence and ask her to marry him.

Pine Ridge Road was a long, rural affair winding north from the village, through the forested valley, past a few isolated houses, to the ski area and beyond. As Nick drove by the cottage with the "Balloon the Berkshires—Office" sign on the front lawn, his thoughts again turned to Chelsea Lawton and their unfortunate meeting at the hospital. At the same time, he reached for the package of antacids on the dash.

It was too bad the encounter turned as negative as it had. He'd really rather liked her before she'd embarked on the touchy subject of hot-air balloons...the healthy glow of her complexion, the fragrance of spring rain in her hair, even the solid weight of her breasts under that voluminous rain gear as she'd bumped into him.

Her eyes, though. He'd never seen eyes that color before, silver-gray that looked like lake water at dawn. It was all he could do to keep from staring. And when they'd been in the waiting room, had she been conscious of his attention? Had she sensed how tightly coiled he was trying to contain his awareness of her? From the way she'd bolted after he'd looked at her that one time, he guessed she had.

Perhaps he shouldn't have reacted so strongly when she'd told him about her business. A simple "No, thanks" would've sufficed. But the thought of Katie's going up in one of those things had short-circuited every synapse in his brain. Polite conversation had become impossible, and abrasiveness had replaced his usual even temper. He'd almost lost his daughter once, and once was quite enough. He'd take no more chances with Katie's life.

Besides, how slight *were* the chances of accidents happening in a hot-air balloon? As far as he knew, human beings had very little control over them. They went wherever the wind took them. He was sure he'd even read accounts of people being killed . . .

No, he'd definitely done the right thing. First reactions were usually the best reactions, and everything inside him had screamed out against this Chelsea taking his daughter for a ride.

The only problem now, however, was that his job was going to be more difficult. After letting the woman know what he thought about ballooning, telling her he needed the property she'd been leasing for the last six years was going to appear like a personal vendetta. Nick drummed his closely trimmed nails on the steering wheel and blew out a long, discontented sigh.

Katie looked at him. "Whatsa matter, Dad?"

Nick pulled himself up sharply. "Nothing, Spud. Nothing."

Within seconds, though, with his words still hanging in the air, everything was the matter. Out in the meadow below Pine Ridge stood Chelsea Lawton and her damn balloon!

Katie drew in her breath with a hitch of excitement. "What's that? Oh, Daddy, look at *that*!"

Fascinated in spite of himself, Nick eased up on the gas. By the time he reached the Balloon the Berkshires billboard, the car was rolling at a snail's pace. He stared out at the huge balloon, a carousel of jewel-toned stripes—red, orange, yellow, green, blue, purple—each gore a different festive color. Seven or eight stories high, it had to be, gently swaying against the clear blue morning sky.

Katie was out of her safety belt and over the seat in a flash, nose pressed hard against the window behind Nick.

Nick had no trouble recognizing the redheaded nurse from the hospital. She was standing inside the wicker basket—good Lord, those things really were just made of wicker!—and she was pulling on something that caused a loud, whooshing flame to shoot up into the dome of nylon.

Chelsea was examining the trailer hitch behind her Jeep, her shapely jeans-clad bottom aimed directly toward the road. Nick sensed she knew he was there, but didn't want to turn around. A dark-haired man wearing glasses was sitting close by on the flatbed trailer hooked to the Jeep. He was leaning toward her, and Nick wondered irritably who he was. His eyes were on Nick's car, and he seemed to be giving Chelsea a furtive blow-by-blow.

"Can we stop, Dad?" Katie pleaded.

But Nick barely heard her. Emotions too confused to sort out were roaring in his ears. He stepped on the gas and sped up the road. He couldn't think about Chelsea Lawton now, nor those enormous gray eyes of hers. Not now, not ever.

CHAPTER THREE

"HOPE HE GOT an eyeful," Chelsea's brother, Larry, drawled as the blue Volvo took off.

"Maybe he was thinking of asking for a ride." Mimi was equally sardonic.

Chelsea felt unaccountably rubber-legged as she straightened and turned. In an abrupt fit of rebelliousness, she made a vigorous arm gesture that would have had her Italian grandfather roaring.

"Ditto!" Mimi seconded with a laugh.

The car glinted and disappeared around a far curve, then reemerged on a high road within the compound of ski buildings. Chelsea squared her shoulders defiantly. It was too nice a day to let Nick Tanner get under her skin.

But he was there nonetheless. Who was he, anyway? Where the devil had he come from? And more importantly, why? Mr. Lockwood had been running Pine Ridge by himself for as long as she could remember.

Maybe she would've gotten some answers if Katie hadn't been so adamant about leaving the hospital the other day, but because of Katie, her conversation with Nick Tanner had ended all too abruptly, leaving her hanging in midspeculation.

From the little that had been said, however, it was obvious that Mr. Tanner did not like hot-air balloons, and the one-month lease still sitting on her desk was beginning to make a horrible sense.

Chelsea hated thinking about their meeting. Her stomach knotted every time she did. The situation wouldn't be half so difficult if their history had begun with Mimi's introducing them. Then the only images haunting her would be those of his being imperious and unreasonable. She could handle that. Unfortunately, they'd met before, and within those ten or twelve previous minutes an entirely different communication had taken place. She knew it was silly to read meaning into so brief a time and so thin a conversation, but knowing didn't make it any easier to forget. Neither did it prevent that small breathless rush whenever she pictured his smile.

"Anyone want coffee?" she called, shaking him off with an effort.

"Yes, please!" Larry answered gratefully.

Larry and Mimi were her crew today, and like her they'd been up since before dawn. But there were no complaints. Larry was a pilot, too, though he still didn't have his own balloon, and many a morning Chelsea had roused herself from bed to crew for him.

Chelsea reached into the Jeep for her thermos and three cups. She wished she were doing a charter today, but all she had was a lesson—Jeff Roche, a cocky seventeen-year-old who insisted on earning his license. Usually she took up a few students at a time. It was more economical that way, and they learned from each other. But today was set aside strictly for Jeff.

"It's getting late, Chelse," Larry said, eyeing the wind sock atop the billboard.

She handed out the steaming cups. "I know."

Ballooning days started early because that's when the air was at its calmest. As the sun rose, so did the wind, and usually ballooning became impossible until dusk, when the winds of the day again died down.

"He should've been here almost an hour ago," Mimi complained. "It isn't fair we do all the work. He should pitch in, too. He's the one who's supposed to be learning."

"I know," Chelsea again replied.

"You shouldn't even be giving him a lesson after the stunt he pulled last week," Larry added.

A smile tugged Chelsea's mouth. "Maybe it'll be the last one he'll need."

Larry squinted at her through his scholarly, steel-rimmed glasses. "What've you got up your sleeve, sis?"

"Nothing!" But she knew that wasn't so. Jeff Roche deserved to be taught a lesson. His indulgent father had already bought him a balloon—brand-new, state-of-the-art—and last week, with only two flight hours under his belt, Jeff had taken a notion to embark on a maiden voyage. By some quirk of fate that protects fools and young children, Chelsea had been driving by his house just as he was about to lift off from the back lawn. She'd been so furious she'd all but knocked him out of the basket. She'd lectured him about the complexity of ballooning and how dangerous it was if a pilot wasn't skilled. She'd also threatened to blacklist him with the licensing board, but she suspected little had sunk in.

"Well, look who's decided to show," Mimi commented.

The teenager skidded his red TransAm into the field and revved the engine irritatingly before turning it off.

"Hey, what's happenin', guys?" he called as he unfolded his long, loose limbs from the car.

Chelsea strode off to the basket, deciding it was better to make herself busy than to start lecturing again. She checked the two safety helmets she'd thrown in earlier, then the instrument panel on the rail. Next she tested the sandbags tied over the side. She almost never resorted to using ballast, but today she suspected it might come in handy.

"Great morning, huh, Chelse?" Jeff grinned as he slid over the rail.

"Wonderful," she replied flatly.

A short time later, the giant balloon was straining to be airborne. Chelsea was about to unclip the tether line, when she spotted something moving through the meadow. She shaded her eyes against the sun. "What the...?"

"My Lord! That's Katie Tanner!" Mimi exclaimed.

Katie came running toward them in her uneven gait, nearly out of breath. An eager smile dimpled her cheeks.

"Katie, what are you doing here?" Chelsea climbed out of the basket, giving the child—and then the empty road— a worried glance.

"I wanted to see," Katie explained, almost falling backward as she gazed up at the towering balloon.

Chelsea looked toward Pine Ridge, dread prickling down her spine. "Does your father know you're here?" She knelt and held the little girl by the waist.

Katie pouted as she pondered an answer. "Yes," she said in an uncertain voice. Chelsea was sure it was a fib.

"Hey, it's time to start," Jeff whined.

Chelsea stood up. "If I were you, Jeff, I wouldn't remind anyone of the time." But she knew he was right. She looked at the others helplessly. "We can't just leave her."

"I'll stay with her," Mimi offered.

"I'm shorthanded today as it is. I can't spare you."

"Can I go for a ride?" Katie asked expectantly.

"Oh, no, honey..." Chelsea answered.

"Why not?"

"You... you just can't."

"Are you going?"

"Yes, I am, but..."

Mimi leaned over. "Katie, remember me?"

Katie remembered all right. The nurse. She scowled, inching closer to Chelsea.

"You walked all the way down from Pine Ridge just to see us?" Mimi tried again.

"No. The balloon."

"All that way. My goodness!" Mimi caught Chelsea's eye and winked. She got the point. Katie wanted to see the balloon so badly she'd walked more than a mile regardless of her leg.

There was little Chelsea could do about that now, however. Katie's father hated balloons, and as pigheaded and self-defeating as his stand was, she knew it was the only stand that mattered. Meanwhile, the sun was getting higher, and clouds were scudding at a worrisome pace.

"There's only one thing we can do," Chelsea decided. "You two will have to take her back to her father. We can't leave her here, and we can't tell her to walk back up the hill. I doubt she'd make it. Take her with you in the Jeep. You'll be going right by the ski area, anyway. Detour in and drop her off. Which building is your father in, Katie?"

Katie didn't seem to like this turn of events. She took a while to answer. "The one with the big windows."

Larry chuckled. "Great. They all have big windows."

Chelsea shrugged. "Do your best. Okay, let's get going." She got into the basket again and fired the burner.

"Be careful, sis," Larry called as the basket lifted.

Slowly, silently, the ground fell away, and up she and Jeff went. Below them, growing ever smaller, Larry, Mimi and Katie were piling into the Jeep.

"What's the weather for today?" Jeff asked offhandedly.

Being apprised of the weather was as natural—and necessary—to a balloonist as breathing. If she'd wanted to, Chelsea could have given Jeff a rundown of every front moving across the country, but today she refused.

"I don't know. Didn't you call the Flight Service Station?" She watched his face drop.

"No. You always do that."

She sat on a tiny corner bench and draped her arms along the rail. "I thought since you've decided you're ready to handle one of these things by yourself, I'd let you."

"Oh, wow!" The young man was thrilled until the reality of his predicament hit home. Chelsea saw alarm visibly tightening his face.

"Jeffrey..." Her voice was deceptively calm as she nodded toward an approaching maple. It was the only tree in the entire meadow, and they were heading straight into it.

"Holy cow!" He lunged for the burner. Fortunately, the blasting flame heated the air inside the envelope quickly enough for them to make a sharp ascent over the obstacle. Chelsea's tense grip loosened on the cord of a sandbag whose release would've lightened their weight and effected the same ascent.

Jeff looked down at her with big, worried eyes. "Should I keep burning?"

"Don't ask me. You're the one running this ship. What do you think?"

"Yeah, I think I should. Yeah." But he wasn't really sure at all. It wasn't going to be an easy day for the young hot-shot. Not if she could help it.

Chelsea picked up the two-way radio. "Larry, you're coming up on the entrance to Pine Ridge. Don't forget Katie."

"I won't. How are things upstairs?"

She glanced at Jeff. Ground heat was already playing havoc with wind currents. He looked a little green around the gills. "Fine. Just fine."

"Well, be careful. You're really clipping along, you know."

Yes, she knew. If this had been a charter, she would've canceled it. But she liked taking her students up in wind. How else were they supposed to gain experience? And she'd certainly flown in worse. Conditions today were manageable, yet they might be enough to scare a little sense into her arrogant student.

They skimmed the ski area, flying so low that they nearly hit one of the huge girderlike chair-lift supports. Only Chelsea's judicious ballasting got them over. They weren't quite so lucky, however, with a stand of trees that separated two ski runs. Small treetop branches went snapping everywhere as they plowed through. Now Jeff was visibly shaken. He turned up the burner until they were at 1,400 feet and too high to hit anything—except erratic wind shears that had even Chelsea chewing her nails.

She leaned over the rail, scanning the public road for the Jeep. But it wasn't there. She found it deep within the Pine Ridge ski area, jouncing over a rutted utility path. Chelsea had to laugh. Chasing a balloon could be an adventure in itself, especially here in the mountains. More often than not, she and her chase cars lost contact with each other entirely. She picked up the radio and asked Larry if he'd dropped off Katie.

"Uh . . . no. I tried to—"

"No! What do you mean, no?"

"I mean she couldn't remember where her father was, and I didn't want to waste any more time looking. I was afraid I'd lose you."

"Jeez, Larry! You've still got the kid?"

"Yep. She's having a ball, too. Thinks this is the best thing since the Bubble Bounce."

"Great. *Now* what are we going to do? It might be an hour before we get back. A parent searching for a missing child could be out of his mind by then."

"That's presuming he's searching."

"You're right. Anyone lax enough to . . ." Realizing that Katie could probably hear their conversation, she kept the rest of her opinion to herself. "Do you suppose Pine Ridge has a radio?'' Even as she was speaking, a familiar car appeared on the road below, following the Jeep. ''Oh, great!''

''What is it, sis?''

''Another car's just joined the chase.''

''Yeah?''

''Yeah. A blue Volvo.''

''Uh-oh. Looks like I should've dropped off the kid.''

''Looks like. What say we call it a day, Lar?''

''Smart call.''

''Smithsons' farm seems a likely spot from where I sit.''

''Roger. Meet you there.''

It was a hair-raising ride, and an even more hair-raising landing. An eight-mile-an-hour wind was Chelsea's ideal flying speed, but today they were coming in at twenty-five. ''Flex your knees, Jeff. Keep them soft,'' she instructed as the field whizzed beneath them.

The basket landed with three teeth-jarring bumps, then lay perfectly calm. The envelope, however, was still partially inflated and moving over their heads. Chelsea had yanked on the rip line to release the air through the port at the crown of the balloon, but it couldn't escape quite fast enough. The slowly collapsing nylon, drifting overhead, suddenly was in a position where it caught the wind just right and puffed like a giant spinnaker, and the basket leapt into the air again. It came down even harder than before, once, twice, then tipped on its side, but even then it wouldn't stop. Before Larry and Mimi could run across the field, Katie in tow, and latch onto the basket, the wind had dragged it almost a hundred feet.

''Are you okay, Chelse?'' Mimi looked ready to cry.

''Oh, sure.'' Chelsea smiled reassuringly as Larry helped her to her feet. ''I've suffered worse.''

A very shaken young man crawled out after her, his thin face pale and lost within the helmet he'd been only too willing to put on. On his hands and knees he seemed to be paying homage to the solid ground.

"How are you, Jeffrey?" Chelsea inquired with perhaps too much satisfaction. She didn't hear his answer, though, because a Volvo was careering to the side of the road.

Nick Tanner crossed the field as if he wanted to kill. Chelsea braced herself, dreading this encounter even more than she'd dreaded the landing.

"What the hell do you think you're doing?" he shouted, even before he'd reached her.

"Good morning to you, too, Mr. Tanner."

"I'll give you a good morning! Of all the lamebrained stunts . . . Miss Lawton, are you totally off your rocker?"

Chelsea bit back the angry words that wanted to leap off her tongue. "Please calm down, Mr. Tanner. As you can see, everyone here is fine."

"Fine? Fine?" He flailed his arms. "I've never seen such an irresponsible operation in all my life!"

Larry was by Chelsea's side in a flash, eyeing Nick coldly. "Anything I can do for you?"

"Larry, it's okay. I can handle this."

"It's no bother."

"Really, Larry. Go. They need you." She hooked a thumb toward the balloon.

"All right. But if he gives you any lip . . ."

She dealt him a stern look, and he finally walked away.

"Now, Mr. Tanner, you were saying?"

"Yes, Miss Lawton, I was saying . . . Is this a habit of yours, kidnapping seven-year-olds and taking them on reckless joyrides?"

Chelsea's blood boiled. "No, Mr. Tanner. Only those whose parents allow them to wander unsupervised down country roads where cars clip along at sixty miles an hour!"

His eyes turned so fiery that Chelsea took a step back. "I hope you don't expect me to dignify that with an answer."

"No, because I don't think you have one."

"Tell me," he said through teeth that wouldn't unclench, "when were you planning to let me know where she was?"

"Would it have made any difference to you?"

Katie ran up to her father just then and clasped his left hand in both of hers. "Daddy, did you see it?"

"Are you okay, baby?" His gentleness surprised Chelsea.

"'Course I'm okay. Did you see it, Dad? Come see it."

"Wait a minute, Katie."

But Katie couldn't wait. She ran back to Mimi, Larry and a somewhat recovered Jeff, who were dismantling the balloon.

"We could've left your daughter back in the field, you know," Chelsea resumed. "We didn't have to bring her with us."

"I don't see how what you did was any better."

"Oh, so you're saying we should've let her walk back to Pine Ridge on her own?" She laughed incredulously. "You really are a piece of work!"

"Don't put words in my mouth. I never said I wanted you to abandon her. But taking her all over creation in an open Jeep? She could've been seriously hurt. I ought to sue you."

Sue her? Chelsea gulped. Angry as she was, those words terrified her. Did he have grounds for a suit?

"M-my crew is extremely capable, Mr. Tanner. They know exactly what they're doing."

"I doubt that very much, and I doubt you do, either. Do you realize you almost hit a ski lift back there?" He pointed furiously. "And the way you landed... Is that how you land one of those damn contraptions?" He leaned closer, his anger pressing down on her. "Then you wonder why I don't want you taking my daughter for a ride!"

"Mr. Tanner, you're being unfair. If you'd let me explain—"

"Unfair?" His eyes seemed to spit fire. "Oh, no. What I am is shocked, shocked that you're allowed to take innocent children up in that thing, shocked that you're allowed to operate at all!"

"Mr. Tanner, that wasn't a typical landing. If you knew anything about me, you'd realize—"

"I've seen quite enough, thank you." He took a determined step past her. "Katie!" he called, but a moment later he turned, recapturing her in his steel-trap stare. "Do you use Pine Ridge land every time you go ballooning? Even when you take kids up on your charity missions?"

Chelsea felt cornered, an image of her new lease flashing across her mind. "Most of the time."

He nodded to private voices, his eyes condemning her. Then, "Katie!"

The child was helping squeeze out the last of the air trapped in the envelope. Her arms were wrapped around the nylon, now just a long, compressed tube, and she was digging in her heels as she slid the bubble from one end to the other.

"Come on, Katie."

She looked over, her cheeks rosy from her labors. "Do I hafta?"

"Yes, you hafta. Let's go, young lady."

Everyone bid her goodbye as she hobbled away. They had enjoyed her company, but Chelsea sensed the others were as eager as she to see Nick Tanner leave.

"What a jerk," Larry muttered as he came to stand beside Chelsea.

"Double-jerk," Mimi said. "Even if he is kind of sexy."

"Mimi!" both Larry and Chelsea groaned.

"Well, he is."

Chelsea wished she didn't agree, but as infuriating as he'd been and as harried as she felt, she still had to admit the man was a powder keg of sensuality.

She only wished her home and business weren't sitting atop that keg, ready to blow.

CHAPTER FOUR

ON MONDAY MORNING the telephone rang in the main office at Pine Ridge, interrupting the informal conference between Nick Tanner, Chet Lockwood and a young architect.

"Excuse me," Chet said, extending his beefy hand toward the receiver. "Why, hello, Chelsea. How are you?"

Nick's eyes snapped up from the blueprints laid out on Chet's desk. He felt his heartbeat quicken.

"I was afraid you might worry about that change in your lease," Chet continued.

Nick pretended to study the plans, but his mind had returned to Saturday morning and his argument with Chelsea Lawton out in that field. He didn't blow up often these days. He used to, those months after Katie's accident. At doctors and nurses, even at hospital orderlies. In his anxiety over Katie's slow recovery, his sense of protectiveness had turned fierce.

He supposed that's what had happened again on Saturday—which was understandable. He'd panicked when he'd realized Katie was missing. He'd run in circles, calling for her, fighting off visions of her lying hurt somewhere. How had he let it happen? His carelessness enraged him. He should've kept her indoors. He should've hired a sitter. He should've done something. But he hadn't. He'd failed—again.

Then *it* had appeared, the balloon, and he'd intuitively known it was linked to Katie's disappearance. A moment later he'd spotted his daughter bouncing along in that open

Jeep, and he'd gone berserk. He'd wanted to tear Chelsea Lawton limb from limb.

Nick's attention returned to Chet's phone conversation.

"I'm sorry I didn't call and explain. I should have, but things've been really hectic around here lately. I've taken on a new partner.... Oh, you've heard?"

Nick waited, wondering if Chelsea would say anything about having met him already. From the ensuing conversation, he guessed she chose not to, which was what he'd been hoping.

He'd obviously made the right decision refusing to let Katie take a ride with her. She was so inept at ballooning she almost felt embarrassed for her. And he wasn't sorry he'd blown up after she'd landed. She'd deserved it, and more.

What he didn't feel comfortable with, though, was the concern he'd felt as he'd watched that small basket hurtling across the field. Concern? No. Dread was more like it. Helplessness. Familiar dark echoes from his life with Laura.

That had been the worst part of loving Laura. He'd never gotten used to living on the edge of disaster. The sweats, the nightmares, the desperate lovemaking before a race. Then there were the arguments and threats. He didn't need that anymore. He didn't need any of it, and why he'd felt that old familiar knife in his chest on Saturday morning was a mystery. Chelsea Lawton meant nothing to him, and never would.

"Listen, Chelsea ..." Chet's voice drew Nick out of his bleak thoughts. "How about coming by the house tonight?"

Nick nearly tipped the coffee mug he was lifting.

"I'd like to tell you all about what's happening at Pine Ridge. It's exciting. Besides, we haven't seen you in ages. Grace'll be so pleased. You girls never get together anymore."

Nick swallowed his coffee with a loud gulp. Good Lord! Chelsea and Grace were friends?

"Yes, eight o'clock's fine. See you then."

So, Chelsea was paying them a call tonight? Well, fine, Nick decided. He would be polite, but he'd also be firm. It was time Chelsea was apprised of the situation. She'd probably be upset, but business was business. Besides, Katie didn't need to have temptation constantly sailing over her head, and he certainly didn't want any more trees pruned. He was having fits as it was, thinking about liability insurance and whether Chet had bothered to cover Pine Ridge against this gray-eyed threat to his peace of mind.

Nick looked thoughtfully at the blueprints as the architect resumed conversation, but it was a long while before he heard a word he said.

CHELSEA TOOK ONE MORE calming breath before ringing the bell. She was glad to be here, she reminded herself. She needed to find out what this one-month nonsense was all about. But the truth was she didn't want to hear it. If Nick Tanner was involved, the news was bound to be bad.

She stepped back to admire the graceful, fanlighted door—and to get her mind off the reason for this visit. The Lockwoods lived in a classic Federal-style house, built in the late 1700s. The Age of Reason, Chelsea recalled, an age of order, irrefutable laws of nature and Ben Franklin's neat aphorisms. She appreciated the place on an objective level, but personally it had always made her edgy. With its perfectly balanced windows and rooms, its stiff period furniture and dour portraits arranged just so, it always seemed to be lecturing: a place for everything and everything in its place. It had been Mrs. Lockwood's ancestral home. She'd loved it, as Grace did now.

Chelsea was thinking about how different her own house was—quirky, unplanned, but always comfortable—when Grace Lockwood opened the door.

"Chelsea, how good to see you. Come in."

It was remarkable how little Grace had changed since high school. The same timeless shirtwaists, same timeless pumps. Chelsea had always thought Grace had a certain natural beauty, with her ivory complexion and classically styled, soft-brown hair.

Unfortunately, most other people back in school didn't agree. They'd cruelly dubbed her The Stick, a name that referred to her too-thin, ramrod-straight figure and her inflexibly conservative attitudes toward just about everything.

She and Chelsea had never really been friends, just classmates, but the few times Chelsea had stopped by to visit had apparently convinced Grace that they were. That bothered her. She wasn't sure she liked Grace all that much.

"What have you been up to lately?" Chelsea asked, slipping off her jacket.

"Oh, I've been busy, housekeeping for Dad, you know."

Chelsea wasn't surprised. Grace was a consummate homebody. She'd majored in education in college and had tried her hand at teaching for a while. But, as her father phrased it, Grace was a delicate girl who couldn't take much stimulation. She'd quit after a year and hadn't gone out to work since.

"We have houseguests, too, so I've been doubly busy," she added, hanging Chelsea's jacket in the hall closet. "Come on. Everyone's in the living room."

Chelsea was aware of the ticking of the grandfather clock as she entered the room, and then almost immediately her gaze zeroed in on the man who dominated that room. Her heart leapt to her throat.

"Hello, Chelsea," Chet Lockwood said, greeting her from somewhere off to one side, but her eyes were still locked on Nick Tanner. Why was this dreadful man here? Why was he so intent on making her life a living hell?

And why couldn't she stop her pulse from racing whenever he was near?

Slowly, Nick stood up, his gaze pouring over her with a simmering intensity that told her he'd forgotten none of the fireworks of their previous meetings.

Chelsea shook off her dismay and turned to greet her host. "Mr. Lockwood..." She tried to smile.

"Come in, come in." He took her arm and led her forward. Chet Lockwood had been a professional skier in his youth, but in spite of the fact that he still gave lessons, he'd grown rather portly over the years, his girth accentuated by the brightly patterned sweaters he usually wore. His broad face was ruddy from the winter sun, and a shock of white hair overhung his brow like a snowdrift.

"Chelsea, I'd like you to meet my new partner—Nick Tanner."

She reached out and grazed Nick's hand in a semblance of politeness. Brief as the contact was, her palm felt afire when she pulled it away.

"The balloon lady!" Katie's voice suddenly rang out. "Oh, neat!" Katie was sitting cross-legged on the Oriental rug with a coloring book and crayons.

"Hi, Katie."

Chet Lockwood reared back. "What's this? You two... Have you...?"

Nick nodded. "Yes, we've already had the pleasure." His eyes avoided Chelsea's. "Just briefly though. What did you say your name was again?"

So, that's how it was going to be, was it? "Chelsea," she said. "Chelsea Lawton."

"Ah." He nodded and smiled congenially, but she wasn't fooled. He was wound as tight as a clock spring.

As was she. She'd come here to talk to Mr. Lockwood. She hadn't expected to get Nick Tanner in the bargain. This was going to be some evening, she thought.

"Have a seat, Chelsea," Chet invited. "What can Grace get for you? A mixed drink? Wine? Brandy?"

Chelsea agreed to a brandy. She settled onto the couch, feeling unaccountably fragile.

On the way to the liquor cabinet, Grace scooped up the half-full glass beside Nick's chair. "Let me just freshen this for you, Nickie."

Nickie? Chelsea blinked her eyes wide open. The man sitting across the room was a lot of things, but a Nickie he was not. He might be Nick Tanner, private eye. Or Nicholas Tanner, star of stage and screen. But...Nickie?

Grace was back in a flash. "Here you go."

"Thank you." Chelsea watched Grace flutter onto a hassock with a great deal of skirt rustling and hair flipping.

"I need more soda. And a cookie," Katie said rather demandingly, Chelsea thought, and immediately Grace was on her feet again—smiling.

Nick sighed. "I'll go this time."

After Grace resettled herself, Chelsea asked, "Are Katie and Nick the houseguests you mentioned?"

"They sure are. They've been with us for two weeks."

"It's only until I find a place of my own," Nick said, returning from the kitchen, "which I hope'll be soon. I hate imposing."

"Oh, hush up. We'd be insulted if you didn't stay." Grace smiled and tried to hold Nick's gaze. "It's so much fun having people besides Father to look after. I personally hope you don't find a place for months, Nickie."

Chelsea realized she was staring at Grace, dumbstruck. The Stick was openly flirting. Not that Chelsea found the idea of someone flirting with Nick unlikely. It probably happened all the time. But Grace?

She shook her head as if to shake off her distaste and turned, only to find Nick Tanner watching her. But she refused to give in to the nervous flutters he caused.

"You're not from this area, then, Mr. Tanner?"

"No, I'm from Boston. How about you?"

Mr. Lockwood interrupted. "Tell me how you two met. I'm curious to hear how you and Nick know each other."

Nick's eyes met Chelsea's, and for one breathless moment she sensed he was thinking about their collision in the hospital entryway, when the slush on her poncho had slid to his shoes, when they'd smiled and said something about April and she'd found him so inexplicably wonderful.

"We, uh, met at the hospital last week when Katie went in for therapy," Nick finally answered matter-of-factly.

And Chelsea added, "I was there to pick up my sister-in-law. She's a nurse. She introduced us."

"Ah, I see." Chet nodded and sipped his drink. "That would be Larry's wife, right?"

"Right."

"I saw the article in the paper about him a few months ago. Local science teacher gets his balloon pilot's license."

Chelsea was relieved that Mr. Lockwood was satisfied with their sketchy explanation and had moved on.

He half turned toward Nick. "After you're settled into the area, you'll get to know Chelsea and her family better. Crazy about balloons, all of them. For generations back."

Nick's hazel eyes glinted with cool mockery. "That so? And what was it that turned you all so...crazy?"

Chelsea sipped her brandy and counted to ten. "My grandfather. We caught the bug from him. He used to fly gas balloons as far back as the thirties."

"The old man lived with Chelsea's family for a few years. After her father died," Chet explained. "You were what, Chelsea? Ten? Twelve?"

Katie's head was swiveling from one adult to the other, her impish face alight with interest. "Did your mommy die, too?" she asked.

Chelsea flinched, wondering what Katie could possibly be thinking. "No, honey. She's living in Florida."

"What a crazy coot he was!" Chet said, still stuck on Chelsea's grandfather. "He went around in this beat-up old aviator's jacket, even in summer, and he had two fingers missing on one hand. Isn't that right, Chelsea?"

She swallowed hard before nodding. "He lost them to frostbite."

"Yes, but tell Nick where he got that frostbite," Chet urged, leaning forward.

Nick Tanner already thought she was crazy and irresponsible. Now he would think her whole family was, too. "He was at a very high altitude," she said softly.

"I heard him tell the story myself," Chet interrupted, laughing again. "The old coot was so high up, there was barely any oxygen to breathe. He kept blacking out, his instruments were frozen, his ears were bleeding . . ."

"Oh, stop!" Grace shuddered.

Chelsea flicked a glance toward Nick again, feeling his disapproval deepen. Her grandfather had been such a brave man, risking his life to gather data about the atmosphere. And true, he'd been something of an adventurer, as she supposed all balloonists must be, but he'd also been an expert at what he did. He'd taught her everything he knew. He'd been there when she'd earned her license at seventeen, and when he'd died a year later it was to Chelsea that he'd left his equipment.

But the legacy she valued most was not the equipment, though that had helped tremendously in getting her business started. What she really valued was his giving her the sense of beauty he'd felt in flying, the peace and poetry of it. It had helped her weather the harsh uncertainties after her father's death, and innumerable calamities since. And suddenly she wished with all her heart she could explain this to Nick Tanner.

Neither Chelsea nor anyone else got to say another word about her grandfather, however, because Katie suddenly blurted, "I chased Chelsea's balloon."

"What did you say, sweetie?" Grace's voice was nettled silk.

Katie moved her book and crayons onto the couch, settling herself close to Chelsea. "I followed her balloon. In the Jeep."

Grace's pale blue eyes lifted to Chelsea's, demanding an explanation. They unsettled her, these seemingly weak eyes with underpinnings of steel.

"Long story, Grace. Katie spotted us in the field Saturday as we were getting ready, and she walked down from Pine Ridge to get a better look."

"Oh, no!" Grace was horrified. "Nickie? What's this all about?"

Nick shifted in his chair, looking terribly uncomfortable, which caused Chelsea to wonder what Grace's hold on him was.

"She . . . got away. One minute she was playing right outside my office, the next she was gone." His composure shuddered for a moment, and Chelsea realized it wasn't Grace; Nick was shaken over losing Katie. Until that moment she hadn't realized how deeply.

Grace turned stiffly.

"Uh-oh," Katie whispered.

"Katie, you mustn't ever do that," said Grace. "You must always let your father, or whoever is taking care of you, know where you are. You could get hurt wandering off like that. You could get lost. It's naughty.''

Katie ducked her head and concentrated on the page she was coloring. Chelsea's heart ached for her. Grace had always been a bit of a pedagogue. The editorials she remembered her writing for the high-school newspaper had strutted with sanctimony. But, for heaven's sake, she and Katie weren't even related. What right did she have scolding her? Instinctively, Chelsea moved her arm along the back of the couch.

But then she heard Katie rasp a heartfelt swearword under her breath, and she found herself struggling to suppress a grin. Part of her knew that Katie shouldn't be swearing, yet another part applauded her spunk.

"It turned out all right in the end," Chelsea went on quickly. "We didn't want to leave her alone in the field, so Larry took her on the chase, fully intending to drop her off at Pine Ridge on the way. But Katie couldn't remember where her father was, and they couldn't spend any more time looking. I was getting too far ahead...." Chelsea dared a glance in Nick's direction. There. At least Larry's actions were accounted for. Now if only she could explain her own.

"I squeezed the air out, too. I was a lotta help, wasn't I, Chelsea?"

"You sure were, kiddo."

"Oh, Chelsea!" Grace dropped her arms with a plop. "No wonder the poor child was exhausted that day. Remember, Dad? She was already asleep when we came in from the wedding. She was so flushed, too. I became quite alarmed."

Now Chelsea became alarmed. "Was she okay?"

"Obviously, she overdid it. Don't you realize she's handicapped?"

Chelsea winced, and for a moment she thought she sensed a similar reaction flash through Nick Tanner, though it passed so quickly she couldn't be certain. Handicapped. She hated that term. Applied to Katie, sitting right here, she found it especially offensive. Still, Grace did seem genuinely concerned. Maybe she'd underestimated Katie's injury. Maybe she'd blundered by allowing her to join in the work. Katie had appeared to be having such a good time, though. The thought of stopping her had never entered Chelsea's mind.

She was aware of Nick watching her again, studying the changing expressions of her face, of her eyes. Was he glad she'd been put on the defensive? She couldn't tell. She only knew his stare was making her dizzy.

"Want to color with me, Chelsea?" Katie whispered.

"Sure." Chelsea was thankful for the diversion. Katie moved the book so that it spread across both their laps.

"Tell me about this new partnership, Mr. Lockwood," Chelsea said, suddenly wanting to hear whatever she'd come here to learn and be on her way. "As you can imagine, I was really surprised when I heard about it."

"Most people are. I've run Pine Ridge for twenty years alone."

"So, why now? What's up?"

Chet chuckled mirthlessly. "Not profits, unfortunately. Oh, I know we seem to be doing all right, but every year for the last eight, we've lost ground. I guess my mind's been out on the slopes when it should've been on the books."

Nick leaned forward, eager to take over. "Pine Ridge has the potential for being one of the best ski areas in the region, but unless something is done soon to improve facilities and expand, it'll get buried in the competition."

"That's why I asked Nick to come aboard," Chet said. "I can't do it alone. Frankly, I don't know how."

"Actually," Grace supplied, "it was my brother, Fred, who asked. He's the one who introduced us all. He and Nickie worked together in Boston."

Chelsea reached down into memory. "Investment banking. Isn't that what Fred went into?"

"That's right." Grace sipped her sherry and smiled beatifically. "Father was really lucky to get Nickie. Fred says he's a financial genius."

Ah, so that was his line. Nickie Tanner, Financial Genius. Chelsea glanced up from her coloring. Now the clothes made sense. Even tonight, an ordinary Monday, he was wearing a dress shirt and tie. Still, Nick Tanner didn't strike her as a banker. His hair was a tad too long, and his pants, those expensive, knife-creased trousers, hugged his hips with a sensuality no self-respecting banker would ever admit to.

Katie was giggling now, pressing warmly against Chelsea's arm as she watched her color. For the moment, Chelsea forgot her uneasiness and enjoyed this adorable child's laugh.

"Oh, Chelsea, honestly!" Grace said.

She looked up, startled. Grace's face registered genuine horror. Chelsea looked at her page, then up again. Evidently, Grace believed there was only one way to color, to the rules and without imagination.

"They're aliens, Grace. From the planet—uh...Zingador. Everybody knows Zingadoreans have purple skin. So, Nick," Chelsea rushed on, ignoring Grace's disapproval, "you and Fred worked together?"

"Yes, for several years."

"Did you like investment banking?" Talking to Nick wasn't all that hard as long as she had an excuse not to look at him.

"Not very much, but I didn't know it for a long time."

"He was too busy being good at it," Grace intervened. Then, "Oh, for heaven's sake, Chelsea! Now you've got the child doing it!" Her voice was shrill with outrage.

Katie's head jerked up, her expressive blue eyes dark with embarrassment and confusion.

"Let's see what you've done, Katie," Chelsea murmured. "Hmm. Orange faces. Blue hair. These must be Bangadooleans."

"Yes, they are," Katie asserted gleefully.

"Well, I think you've done a magnificent job."

"Oh, thank you. I think so, too." Katie then glowered at Grace, who had gone quite red.

Chelsea swore she caught Nick trying to fend off a smile. As she watched him, one tugged at her own lips, too.

She cleared her throat and glanced at the crayon box, instead. "So, Mr. Tanner, did you just up and quit the bank one day to take on a ski area?"

"Yes. And no. Fred knew I'd been hoping to get into a business of my own for a while. I had money to invest, and the know-how. So he mentioned that his father was having difficulties with the ski area and asked if I'd be interested in getting involved."

"Do you have any experience in the ski business?"

"Not much. I ski a little."

"Learns damn fast, too," Chet Lockwood offered. "Nick knows as much as I do already."

"Hardly. But I'm here to manage finances, not to make decisions about ski bindings. Chet's the expert in that department."

Chet smiled appreciatively. "What I really like about Nick is he's got the courage to take chances. He's a real firebrand, Chelsea. In five years, you won't recognize Pine Ridge."

Waves of apprehension prickled up her back. "Really. What exactly do you have in mind?"

"Nothing that Chet didn't think of himself. Years ago he had an engineering team survey the south peak. He's always known he could cut trails there. Ten or twelve new runs."

The prickles were becoming decidedly uncomfortable now.

"The trouble was," Chet said, taking over, "I never had the capital for such an expensive project, and I was afraid to take loans. But now..." He smiled with humble gratitude.

"Well, it sounds wonderful. I wish you all the best." Chelsea supposed she meant it sincerely. After all, the more Pine Ridge expanded, the more potential customers she'd have.

Chet Lockwood looked uneasy. He rattled the ice cubes in his glass, then got up and made a fresh drink. "If we go through with this project..."

"You mean *when*, Chet," Nick amended.

"Yes, of course." He turned from the liquor cabinet. "Here comes the hard part, Chelsea."

"Yes? What?"

"We're going to need the meadow you're using."

"The meadow. My meadow?" That wasn't what she'd expected. She'd expected Chet to say Nick was making him raise her rent.

"That meadow," Nick explained with none of Chet's uneasiness, "forms a natural basin to the south peak."

"I realize that, but how much land do you need? Lifts don't take up that much space."

"Lifts are the least of it," Grace put in excitedly. "Nickie has come up with an idea for a whole ski village."

"A village!"

Nick's cool, restrained stare was unswerving. "That's right. Pine Ridge doesn't provide on-site lodging. It loses a lot of business because of that."

Chelsea moved to the edge of the cushion. "S-so, what are you talking about? Condos? Rental units?"

"Both." He looked relaxed and fully in control.

"Stores, too," Grace added. "Gift shops, boutiques—you know, the kinds of places tourists love to browse through."

So, Nick Tanner was really a developer, bane of balloonists everywhere!

"We'd like to have a cross-country center there, too," Chet elaborated, eyes alight with enthusiasm. "And just this morning we were talking about adding sleigh rides."

Chelsea swallowed over a lump in her throat. "I guess what you're telling me is I'd better look for a new field."

Chet nodded into his drink, his broad face flushed.

Chelsea's foot tapped a tight staccato. She couldn't lose that field. She couldn't. "Mr. Tanner, hot-air balloons happen to be a big attraction these days. They're bright and festive, and people have a natural fascination with them."

Nick frowned. "What's your point?"

"My point is, I think you should consider the number of skiers who return to Pine Ridge precisely because of the festive atmosphere we lend, or... or because they want to take a balloon ride. And how about all those people who come to take a ride and then decide to stay and ski? How about that?"

Nick stared back at her, calm and unmoved. "A symbiotic relationship, is that how you see it?"

"Yes."

"As I see it, the scales are tipped steeply in your favor. More a parasitic relationship, don't you think, Miss Lawton?"

"I beg your pardon?"

"Please, don't take it personally. It's simply an empirical fact. Anybody can see you benefit far more from being located near us than we do from being near you."

Chelsea rose half-out of her seat before remembering she was a guest in this house. She sat back, but she wouldn't let the comment pass. "Let's be honest, Mr. Tanner. You just don't want me anywhere near Pine Ridge."

"I never said that." Nick sounded sincere, but she noticed his eyes avoided hers. "And I didn't mean to upset you."

"What did you mean, then?"

"I was hoping you'd understand how important it is for Pine Ridge to expand. The truth is it won't survive another two years unless it does, and the real estate you're using is vital to our plan."

The room had fallen unbearably quiet. Even little Katie was stiff and silent by Chelsea's side.

"When does construction begin?"

Nick shrugged. "Construction dates are still uncertain. That's why we don't want to commit ourselves to any long-term contracts. In all likelihood, we'll be able to offer you another one-month lease after this one expires."

Chelsea squared her shoulders. "And after that?"

"I can't see that far ahead."

Chelsea's throat ached. She had her answer.

"Oh, there's something else," Nick said. "Your house."

"My house?"

"Yes. We're going to need that, too."

Chelsea stopped breathing. She couldn't move or think.

Chet Lockwood looked genuinely distressed now. "Chelsea, will it be that much of a hardship to find another place?"

Chelsea felt bad for him, but worse for herself. "No, of course not." It was a bald lie.

"Good. I thought as much."

"There's one other matter," Nick cut in. "Your billboard."

Chelsea's sigh came from her toes. "Of course. I'll move it." How and where, she had no idea.

"If there's anything I can do..." Chet offered.

She attempted a smile and got to her feet. She had to get out of here. "Thanks. But there's nothing."

"You're not going yet, are you?" Grace asked.

"Yes, afraid I have to. I have a charter tomorrow at dawn. A couple celebrating their twenty-fifth anniversary."

Chet crossed the room and hugged her. "Glad you dropped by." He seemed relieved to have this evening behind him.

"Chelsea, here. Would you like my picture?" Katie held up the colored page, which she'd torn from the book.

"You mean it? I can really have it?"

The little girl beamed.

"You'll have to sign it, though. An artist should always sign her work."

"Oh." Katie bit her lip in concentration as she chose a crayon.

The room was tense, too quiet. "What school will she be going to?" Chelsea asked to fill the void.

"She . . . isn't," Nick answered.

Grace rushed in with an explanation. "Nickie's decided to keep her home awhile. I'm going to tutor her."

Chelsea suspected she was frowning. Fiercely.

"Here ya go," Katie sang.

Chelsea took the page, then watched Nick lift Katie into his arms and step back. The gesture was perfectly normal—a father holding his little girl as they all said goodnight—yet it struck a strange chord. Chelsea had the oddest feeling he was trying to protect his daughter. From her.

"I hope you won't hold a grudge against Father," Grace whispered out in the hall.

"How could I? He's always been very kind."

"But you *are* upset. Because of Nickie. Don't think ill of him, Chelsea. He was a bit rough on you, but, well . . .

sometimes he gets that way. It's understandable with all he's been through the last few years.''

Chelsea rubbed her forehead, trying to ease the dull pounding behind her eyes. "What do you mean, Grace?"

"The accident, of course."

"The one that hurt Katie's leg?"

Grace nodded. "And killed her mother."

"Killed...what?"

"Didn't you know?"

"No. I'd heard she was dead, but I didn't realize... Oh, how awful!" The hall began to sway as another thought struck her. "Was it a car accident? Was Nick driving?"

"Heavens, no. It was Katie's mother. She lost control of her motorcycle and went down an embankment."

"Motorcycle?"

"Uh-huh. Do you believe it? She must've been a real nut. She used to compete in semipro races. Nickie fought with her about it all the time. He had a very unhappy marriage, you know. Not that he talks about it, but my brother's told me stories. She wasn't much of a wife, either. You can't imagine how appreciative Nickie is of the simplest home-cooked food." Grace tossed her head. "Just as well she's dead. She caused him nothing but misery."

Chelsea knew she and Nick had their differences, but she couldn't understand how Grace could say such a thing. Losing a wife, having his daughter injured in the same accident... Chelsea felt unaccountably sad for his troubled past.

Suddenly Chelsea remembered how fierce he'd been last Saturday morning, charging across the field, and just as suddenly she understood. In his eyes, she'd represented a threat to Katie. She'd known it then, but not why or how deep into his heart that threat reached. Not till now. Good Lord! He associated her with his wife!

Chelsea's headache was growing worse; even her eyes were throbbing now. She squinted at Grace—so calm, so plain and conservative. So safe!

"Grace, do you mind if I ask you a personal question? Are you and Nick dating?"

"Well, of course. Isn't it obvious?"

Chelsea's mouth dried to cotton. "Oh, sure, I could see it right away." She gulped. "Is it serious?"

"I think so."

"Marriage?"

"Well . . ." Grace shrugged and laughed.

Chelsea wanted to say she was happy for Grace, but the words wouldn't come. Suddenly she felt she would explode with the feelings swelling inside her.

"Well, thanks for having me over." She opened the door and hurried out, needing to drink in the cool night air.

Chelsea couldn't reach her Jeep fast enough. She didn't understand why she was rattled by the news that Nick Tanner was seeing someone. She wasn't looking for a relationship, and certainly not one with him! She disliked the man thoroughly. He was close-minded and contentious, and if that wasn't enough, he was dismantling her life. He could go out with anyone he chose, she didn't care!

But as she drove away from the Lockwood home, Chelsea felt an ache deep inside her, and she knew she did care. A lot.

CHAPTER FIVE

NICK STOOD at the floor-to-ceiling window of his office above the ski-rental shop and listened. He imagined that during winter the thumping of ski boots and din of conversation rising from below would be murder, but for now the only sound was the warm whooshing of the May breeze through the pines. And Katie's singing as she played beneath those pines. From here he could see the base lodge, a bit of the parking lot and a few of the wide green swaths that, in another season, were ski trails. A ski area without snow was always a jolt to the system, especially an area so fragrant and bursting with spring.

Nick's dark brows lowered until they almost met. It had been years since he'd been aware of the sweet smell of spring, the gold-green translucence of new birch leaves, the lift of hope in a robin's song. He'd lived with a dead weight in his soul for so long he'd forgotten there was any other way to feel.

Of course, he'd hoped for a change. That was why he'd moved to the Berkshires. Until now, however, he'd only thought of the move as affecting Katie. He'd wanted to get her away from the pollution and crime and frenetic pace of the big city, give her room and time to grow. He'd never anticipated that the move might have an effect on him, too.

Sure, he'd expected to enjoy his new work, enjoy living without noise and traffic jams. But something else was happening here. Perceptions were sharpening, veils lifting. He felt like a man awakening from a drugged sleep.

Nick ran a slightly unsteady hand through his hair. He wasn't sure he liked it—even if it was just an awareness of robins and new leaves. He wasn't ready. The optimism invading his heart frightened him. Good things in life were fleeting, ephemeral. They always set you up for a fall. Laura had taught him that.

He didn't regret the move, and for Katie's sake he never would. He only wished he didn't feel quite so vulnerable all of a sudden. Ironic as the fact was, part of him wanted to crawl back into that cave of emotional numbness that had enveloped him after Laura's death. It was safe there. He ran no risks of being hurt again.

The sound of an engine shifting gears broke his train of thought. He and Chet had an interview today with a young guy from Colorado, a prime prospect for the job of head ski instructor at Pine Ridge. Nick craned his neck until he spotted the vehicle breezing along the entrance road into the base area—a late-model, open-topped Jeep. His hands splayed out on the sun-warmed glass as he leaned forward. No, it wasn't the new ski instructor. It was Chelsea Lawton!

Chelsea brought her Jeep to a neat stop below his window. He jerked back just as she looked up. With hands that suddenly felt useless, he tucked in his shirt, then made a hasty pass at his hair.

He could hear her talking, could hear her easy, infectious laughter. He edged toward the window again. She was standing in the middle of the hopscotch squares he'd drawn for Katie on the asphalt yesterday, though he doubted she was aware of them. She and Katie, who was now swinging from one of the pine's low branches, were too busy chatting.

Chelsea was wearing a skirt today, a hand-batiked skirt in a shade of lavender that unexpectedly made him think of hyacinths. It was topped by a gauzy lavender and white-lace blouse that fell softly over the curve of her breasts. He liked the outfit. It was different. Homemade, he'd bet. He'd noticed she liked unique things, like the African teak jewelry she'd worn to the Lockwoods' the other night... and those bright blue high-tops last Saturday morning. Nick caught himself smiling in spite of himself.

She was quite a chameleon, changing her appearance as easily as... No, not a chameleon. Chameleons picked up their identity from whatever happened to be near them. But Chelsea Lawton was a woman with a firm grip on who she was and what she liked.

Nick regretted that what she liked included ballooning. He pressed his forehead against the glass and sighed. Odd, he'd sort of been hoping she was better at it....

But that wasn't why he was taking her meadow. He had to. He had no choice.

He was less comfortable about taking the house. He wondered where she would go. It concerned him, which was ridiculous, of course. He didn't give a damn where she went. That was her problem. She'd made her own difficult bed by choosing a ditzy occupation. Besides, she herself had said she'd be all right.

Chet was upset, however, and that upset Nick. Chet obviously liked her. She was a neighbor; Chet knew her family. Grace had even been her classmate.

Nick rubbed a hand over his disgruntled face. He didn't want the Lockwoods to feel guilty or distressed over Chelsea Lawton, but they did, and he'd only exacerbated the situation. He shouldn't have been so abrupt, and he never should have made that comment about her business feeding off Pine Ridge like a parasite. Though it was probably true, it had been low, and he'd only said it because he was still furious over her kidnapping Katie.

Maybe he should apologize. Life with the Lockwoods would be easier if he did. He had no right upsetting a long-time friendship because of personal differences. Yes, he could do that. Then he'd send Miss Lawton on her way, job done and, hopefully, never have to deal with her again.

Chelsea waved to Katie and headed for the steps that led up to Nick's office. As she did, she hopped on one foot down the avenue of hopscotch blocks, 3 - 2 - 1. Her soft lavender skirt flipped gracefully about her shapely legs as she landed squarely on two feet. Nick couldn't help smiling.

There was a lot about Chelsea Lawton he didn't approve of. Her ineptness at what she did for a living. The chances she took with children. The way she reminded him of Laura. But there was no use denying that she was one attractive woman.

He turned and hurried to his desk. By the time she was knocking on his door, Nick had molded his demeanor into a model of indifference.

AT THE TOP of the stairs, Chelsea pulled in a deep breath of courage. She'd been hoping to see Chet Lockwood, but according to Katie only her father was here. Well, fine. She didn't give a hoot. She'd handle Nick Tanner with the same pride and determination that had powered her through her morning.

She'd been driving all over creation placing ads today. Writing out those checks had been painful. Advertising was terribly expensive, but she knew from experience she'd get results. She was tired of driving, tired of talking and shelling out money, but she was also determined to earn some extra money to help get her through the trauma of a move to a new site.

She knocked.

"Come in." It was Nick Tanner's distinctive warm voice.

She squared her shoulders and entered the glass-walled office.

Nick looked up from his desk as if he'd been waiting for her. "What can I do for you, Chelsea?"

Her brisk stride slowed. She hadn't expected to feel so unnerved, but he'd never called her Chelsea before. Not that that should make any difference. He disliked her, she disliked him, and they were both perfectly aware of the situation. She felt almost comfortable with their mutual animosity. At least it was out in the open and recognizable—not like this queazy sense of hanging in space, of not knowing why a simple "Chelsea" should sound so kind.

"I've brought my lease," she began hesitantly. "It's due today. That's why I'm delivering it in person. I thought maybe Mr. Lockwood would be here."

Nick's hazel eyes traveled over her slowly, studying her appearance. She wondered why she'd worn this outfit. It made her look so round and lumpy. And the shoes—to him they probably looked like somebody's grandmother's.

"He hasn't come back from lunch yet. I can take it."

Chelsea walked across the sun-splashed carpet and placed the envelope on the corner of his desk. "He has to sign it."

"I know." Nick's firm, well-shaped mouth twitched for a second. Did he find something about her amusing? "I'll give it to him, I promise."

"Good. I wouldn't want to forfeit the month of May just because I was a day late."

The twitch broadened into a smile. "No one's going to throw you out because you're a day late."

Chelsea glanced away, around the room as if interested in the decor. He was acting awfully strange today.

"Nice office," she said.

"Mmm, I like it. With all these windows, even when I have to be inside, I feel I'm not. Would you like to have a seat?"

"Oh, no, thanks. I should be leaving." But she didn't. She just stood there watching Nick Tanner who was watching her. Unexpectedly, heat bloomed in her cheeks. Good Lord, she thought, it wasn't happening again, was it? The attraction she'd felt for this man last week at the hospital?

In the same instant she corrected herself. The attraction hadn't been isolated to that one afternoon. It had plagued her again that night, lying awake in bed, and at scattered moments every day since. Which was ridiculous. After their run-ins, it made no sense. Besides, he and Grace Lockwood were dating.

"Are you all right?"

"Yes. Sure." She cleared her mind with an effort.

He came around his desk, picking up the envelope she'd placed there.

"About this lease..." He sat on the edge of the desk, tapping the envelope on his muscle-corded thigh. "I hope you realize that none of this mess was directed at you personally."

"Would you blame me if I thought it was?"

"I guess not, considering my behaviour on a few occasions. But you have to believe it wasn't. We simply need that land, Chelsea. We need *that* land, and it wouldn't matter who was on it." There wasn't a trace of mockery left in his voice, and on a sudden wave of insight, Chelsea realized he was apologizing to her. In an oblique sort of way, he was definitely apologizing.

An ironic smile touched her lips. "How did we manage to get off to such a terrible start?"

His head jerked back in pure surprise, and she realized she hadn't meant to say those words out loud. But it was too late. They were already out there in all their raw honesty.

Just then the door opened and Katie came skipping in. "Oops, I forgot to close the door."

"Don't bother, Spud. It's too nice a day. Whatcha got?"

"Pinecones. There are zillions of 'em out there." Her arms were overflowing. "See, Chelsea?" When she raised her arms, a few of the cones and dozens of long, sticky needles slipped to the floor. She tried to catch them, but that only sent the rest of her load tumbling.

Nick groaned. "Oh, Katie! A very important man is going to be here soon." He stooped and hurriedly picked them up. When he went to the wastebasket, Chelsea noticed a few stragglers. She brought them to him, glad he'd gone to the basket only to dig out a crumpled plastic bag.

"Here you go, young lady. Now, go put them out on the deck."

Katie wasn't happy, but she went, anyway.

Nick shook his head. "I should've made her pick them up, shouldn't I? How's she ever going to learn?"

Chelsea had been thinking the same thing herself. He did too much for Katie. "It isn't easy, is it?"

"What?"

"Being a single parent."

"I'll say. Especially to someone like Katie who needs so much special attention."

He was probably right. Still, Chelsea couldn't help feeling that Katie got too much attention—of the wrong kind. He protected her, pampered her—which was understandable because of her accident. But he should stop now. Katie needed to get on with her life. As far as Chelsea could see, she was a strong child, healthy in every way except for her limp. Nick should stop cosseting her weakness. Children knew what kinds of behaviour elicited attention, and if playing helpless was the behaviour that made her father jump, why would Katie act differently?

"Great, now I have pine gum all over my hands." Nick's comment snapped her train of thought. "You, too?"

As Chelsea was examining her hands, Nick reached out and took them in his. The unexpected touch made her breath come up short. For a moment neither of them spoke.

Finally, he drew back. "Yep, just as I thought. Here." He handed her a box of tissues.

She expelled a breath she hadn't been aware of holding. "Thanks, but tissues won't work."

Katie returned. "Let's see your hands, Spud."

The child held them out, palms up. "Uh-oh! I can't go to the hospital now." She shook her head with adult seriousness.

Nick frowned. "What's that, Katie?"

"My hands are too dirty."

"You have therapy today?" Chelsea asked. Katie's answer was a grimace. "I don't think dirty hands matter much at therapy." Chelsea looked at Nick. "Do you have any turpentine? Or paint remover?"

"I doubt it."

"Wait. I may have some nail-polish remover in my bag." She plopped her purse on his cluttered desk and unzipped its many pockets. After a few minutes, Nick began to laugh.

"What haven't you got in there, lady?"

"Don't make fun. Look." She smiled jubilantly as she pulled out a small bottle. She dampened a tissue, then crooked a finger, motioning Katie over. Very gently she rubbed at the sticky black spots. "Okay, go into the bathroom now and wash up, really well, lots of soap."

Lip still jutting out, Katie scuffed her running shoes across the carpet toward the adjoining bathroom.

Chelsea turned to Nick, and the parental warmth that remained in his eyes spilled over on her. She smiled back automatically before self-consciousness won out.

"How was your balloon flight the other morning?"

"Which? The anniversary couple?"

He nodded, taking a freshly moistened tissue from her.

"It was lovely."

"Did...your boyfriend help out that morning, too? Does he usually go along to help?" Nick seemed inordinately taken with his left palm.

"My boyfriend?" She frowned. "Oh! You mean Larry? That guy you met the other day was my brother."

"Ah, I see."

"Ah, you see what?" She didn't know how to interpret the lightning flicker through his features. "I date. I have boyfriends."

"Really." Nick kept rubbing, though the spot was long gone.

"Yes. Several."

"No one special?"

"They're all special."

"Of course."

"Hey, I'm not looking to settle down. Not yet, anyway. I have other fish to fry."

"A career?" His mouth twitched again.

"Precisely." She'd really prefer getting off the subject. To him, her "career" was undoubtedly a joke. "Has Katie been giving you a hard time about therapy?"

"The worst. She hates it, but I hate letting her skip."

"As well you should. Don't let her."

"Easier said than done. Today I may have to. I'm expecting someone this afternoon. His flight's been delayed, and I'm afraid he's going to get here just when I should be leaving with Katie."

"Oh. Can't you reschedule the meeting?"

Nick sat on the edge of his desk again. "If it were anybody else I would, but this guy's flying all the way from Colorado. Looks like it's Katie's session that's got to be rescheduled."

Chelsea chewed on her lower lip, thinking. "But she'll see it as a victory. You'll just be reinforcing her notion that she can hound you until you buckle under." Was this a novel thought? Nick's eyes had a slightly startled look that led her to suspect it was.

He smiled apologetically. "Sorry. I'm sure the last thing you want to hear is a grown man whining about the tribulations of fatherhood."

Or was it rather he didn't want to hear a differing opinion on how to raise his daughter? Chelsea wondered.

"All done, Dad," Katie called from behind them. "My hands are clean, but now my stomach feels funny. I think I want to throw up."

Nick wheeled around. "Katie, enough!"

Katie glowered at him, resentful that he'd seen through her ruse. "I don't want to go. I'm not going." She stamped her foot.

"You are, and that's all there is to it!"

Father and daughter stared hard at each other, locked in impasse. Chelsea wondered if she'd had anything to do with his sudden sternness or if occasionally Katie pushed Nick to the point where even he, the doting protector, realized he had to stand firm.

Suddenly the little girl's jaw trembled and tears filled her eyes. Her brattiness disappeared, giving way to the emotional fatigue and fear that lay beneath it all along.

Nick pulled a hand through his thick hair. "Come here." He lowered himself onto his haunches and held out his arms. Slowly, Katie went to him and let him fold her in his embrace. Chelsea noticed how tired he looked, how distraught his face was, as he pressed it to Katie's soft curls.

"Katie, you're so close," he whispered. "Dr. Green says by September you might be all done. Just a few more months, Spud. I know it's hard, I know."

In spite of herself, Chelsea felt her throat tighten. Raising this little girl wasn't easy. There were no pat answers. "Can I take her?"

Nick looked up, too surprised to answer.

"I mean it. I don't have anything to do this afternoon, and it seems you have too much."

Nick stood to his full height, his hands on Katie's shoulders. "I couldn't let you."

"Why not, for heaven's sake!"

"She's a handful. I wouldn't even let Grace..."

Chelsea's face slowly dropped. Evidently, he thought Grace Lockwood held a monopoly on domestic talents, while all Chelsea Lawton did was fly off into ski lifts. Well, fine! She didn't know why she wanted to help him, anyway.

"I'll go with Chelsea."

Chelsea watched Nick stiffen. They both looked down at Katie, standing between them, her eyes still wet. She was glancing from one to the other, weighing their expressions. "I'll go," she repeated, "*if* I can ride in Chelsea's balloon."

"No!" Nick's answer was a bullet.

Chelsea bit her lip hard to keep from laughing. Even in tears the child was indomitable. "Katie, my balloon isn't going up today, but I have something else you might like."

"What?"

"I can't tell you now, it wouldn't be a surprise. But later on I'll show you, *if* you work real hard at therapy."

The child folded her arms and considered the proposition. "Okay. But it better be good."

"Katie!" Nick reprimanded, trying to arrest his own grin.

"It's settled then. What time is her appointment?"

"Three."

Chelsea strolled toward the door. "Don't worry, she'll be fine. I promise."

Katie scooted between them and down the stairs. They heard her whoop as she clambered into the Jeep.

"Katie, be careful," Nick called out, but then he laughed softly and Chelsea noticed how the laugh transformed his face. He really was a handsome man, she thought. Handsome, and warm—and disturbingly sensual. She'd never met anyone who could turn a simple thing like smiling into a seduction.

He leaned against the doorjamb. "Thanks. I owe you."

"Oh, yeah? Put it in writing." She took in a deep lungful of the sweet, piny air. "Is it my imagination, or are we enjoying a particularly nice spring this year?"

"Funny. I was just thinking that myself."

Chelsea smiled at the sky. She wished she was ballooning today. She wished she could take Katie with her, too. Maybe if Nick got to know her better, realized she wasn't a kook just because her occupation was unusual...

"Hey, do you know where my house is?" The words slipped out spontaneously. "Your house, I mean. The one I live in." He nodded. "Well, instead of my bringing Katie back here and possibly interrupting your meeting, why don't you pick her up when you're ready?"

"I couldn't do that."

"It's no trouble. My two nephews will be there to play with her. And then there are the kittens. That's my big surprise. I know it's not much and you don't like her accepting bribes, but it did seem to appease her."

Nick smiled a lopsided grin that pierced her strangely. "She's going to go nuts. She loves kittens."

"Good, so it's settled. You'll pick her up at my house."

He shrugged defeatedly. "I'll be there as soon as I can."

CHAPTER SIX

NICK PULLED to the side of the road. Besides Chelsea's Jeep, he counted two other cars in her driveway. Did she have company? Well...good. Now he had an excuse to leave right away.

He knew he'd wanted to bridge the gap they'd dug between them. He'd wanted the tension and sharp words to end—for Chet and Grace's sake, of course. And it wasn't that he wasn't grateful to Chelsea for taking Katie off his hands this afternoon. He was. But now that they'd made their peace, he wanted to pull back. He had no intention of becoming any better acquainted with her, and he definitely did not want her to get any closer to Katie. He preferred his daughter get to know women who made a living at something a little less flamboyant than hot-air ballooning. Katie seemed to admire Chelsea far too much as it was. Yes, he was glad things were easier between him and Chelsea, but now it was time to back off.

Chelsea opened the door even as he was knocking. "Hi, Nick."

Nick opened his mouth, then closed it again. He hadn't expected to be so disarmed, but he'd never heard her call him by his first name before. "Uh...sorry I'm late."

"No problem," she said, smiling the most fetching smile he'd ever seen. "Come on in. How'd your meeting go?"

He entered the front hall in the wake of a light, delicious cologne. Or was that just the lingering fragrance of the hyacinths he'd passed on the walk? He was beginning to feel confused.

"It...it went very well. Looks like Pine Ridge is going to have a new ski instructor. How did Katie do?"

"Good. She worked really hard."

"She did?"

"Don't look so surprised. I told you she'd be okay."

Nick had to admit he was surprised. "Oh, here's your copy of the lease. Signed, sealed and now delivered."

"Great. Thanks." Chelsea took the envelope from him, leaned into a room and pitched it toward a desk.

"Your office?"

"Uh-huh."

Nick found himself standing on the room's threshold, soaking in the bright, efficient atmosphere. His gaze roamed slowly, from the deeply cushioned burgundy sofa, over the pale oak desk and files, to the colorful balloon posters decorating the white walls. He nodded in approval. "This... surprises me."

"What, that I have good taste?"

"No." A sheepish grin overtook his expression. "Yes."

"Gee, thanks. Just because I look as if I need someone to dress me doesn't mean I can't hang a decent pair of blinds."

He turned, taking it all in. It was the sort of room that inspired confidence and trust. It clearly said the proprietor here was a professional.

"Did you take these pictures?" he inquired, noticing a group of framed photographs over a bookcase.

"Uh-huh. From my balloon."

"You're very good."

"I try to be. When I'm extra good, people even pay me."

Nick was lost in one of her photographs, taken, it seemed, from the clouds. The sun was just rising, and veils of silver mist were hanging over the dark, gently rolling mountains. He almost didn't hear her. "They pay you?"

"Mmm. Calendar publishers. Local tourist boards looking for postcard material."

Nick swung around to stare at her. "That right? I didn't realize you were so...enterprising." He meant to return to the photo, but now he couldn't take his eyes off her. He'd never seen skin so fresh and smooth, or hair such a deep, shiny brown. And her eyes, those pale gray eyes...

Suddenly Nick was fighting the strangest urge to cross the room and...well...pull her into his arms, crush that gauzy lavender dress against his body...

"Would you like to wait here while I go find Katie?" she asked, spots of color blooming in her cheeks. He wiped a hand over his eyes and made an effort to concentrate. Good Lord! What had he been thinking?

"Wait here? Sure." His disappointment surprised him. She was already shuffling him on his way. But then, wasn't that exactly what he'd wanted—simply to pick up Katie and leave?

He sat on the sofa and tried not to think about Chelsea Lawton. She hurt his head, this woman who crash landed balloons one day and on the next took exquisite pictures— and turned a profit on them, too.

But within seconds he was up and exploring again. On a calendar over her desk, she'd penciled in a smattering of notes. Flight appointments. "Roller skating with boys." What boys? For a moment Nick suffered a vision of her cavorting with dozens of admirers. He sorely hoped "boys" referred to her nephews. Another note, "Hair trim," had been crossed out and replaced with "Pay insurance."

On her desk a newspaper lay open to the job ads, a few circled in red, and in a Lucite bin, a bill for ripstop nylon caught his attention. His heart plummeted when he saw the bottom line. He turned away, telling himself the guilt he felt was only the result of snooping where he had no business. Better to look at those trophies.

They were all Chelsea's, and they all had something to do with ballooning. The dates on them spanned the last eight years, and the places she'd won them ranged from New Mexico to Maine. Nick gazed at the gleaming statuettes and felt increasingly confused.

"Bowling trophies," Chelsea quipped.

He swiveled around at the sound of her voice. "I doubt it," he answered, smiling. He wanted to ask her exactly what she'd done to earn these—and if he was right in suspecting he'd grossly misjudged her abilities. But apparently she preferred to move on.

"Katie wants you to come see the kittens." She looked hesitant. "You don't have to, though, if you don't want to."

"Why would I not want to?"

"My family's here. My brother, Larry, and Mimi, my kid sister, Judy, and her husband, Rob. I don't think you've met them yet."

"I'm sorry. Am I interrupting a special occasion?"

She laughed softly, and Nick discovered he got an immense kick out of the sound. "Yeah. Thursday. It's kind of become a tradition, gathering here for dinner on Thursday."

"I won't keep you then, but I will go and pull Katie away."

"That's what I'm trying to tell you. You can't get to Katie without going through them."

"A gauntlet, huh?" He shrugged. "That's okay."

"You mean it? You don't mind meeting them?"

"Of course not." He rather liked the breathy exuberance that filled her voice every once in a while. "But first you've got to tell me about these trophies."

"You really want to hear it, huh?"

"Go on, serve it up. Crow on a platter."

"They're from various races and competitions I've won at balloon rallies."

"Races? In balloons? It boggles the mind."

"Oh, the competitions aren't for speed. They're for accuracy, for executing certain flight patterns. This one, for instance." She pointed. "I won this by removing a key from the top of a pole. I got to keep what the key unlocked, too— my Jeep."

"Holy... You mean, you won stuff?" Stuff? He groaned inwardly. What a wordsmith he became in her presence!

"Sure. Stuff. Money."

"Holy cow... But wait. What do you mean, accuracy?" He stepped closer, until their arms were just about touching. He'd caught the scent of hyacinths again and wanted more. "You aren't telling me you can steer those things, are you?"

"No, but what we can do is catch wind currents at different altitudes and tack a course accordingly."

"Sounds... tricky."

"It is."

Nick massaged his furrowed brow. Chelsea must be very good then. Very good indeed.

Alongside the trophies, in a frame, was a picture of a long, silver van, its broad side windows revealing rows of plush interior seats. "What's this?" he asked, increasingly fascinated by the room and the things within it.

"Oh, that." She laughed. "That's my inspiration."

"Your... I don't think I understand."

"You would if you saw the van I own now. It's a wreck. Someday I'd like to replace it with this model."

"Oh." But he still didn't understand. Ballooning couldn't pay that well, could it? That van seemed a costly indulgence.

She must have sensed his confusion. "A van's imperative in my line of work. I don't think I've ever had a charter where my passengers were the only people who showed up. They always bring relatives or friends who want to tag along on the chase. Then, of course, when the flight's done, we all have to be carted back to our take-off point." She sighed, staring longingly at the expensive vehicle. "Okay, enough of this. Let's go start that gauntlet."

He followed her down the hall, through a well-lived-in sitting room and across a dining room. "They're all in there, in the kitchen," she warned.

Nick didn't expect the kick of adrenaline he experienced. Quickly, he combed back his hair with both hands.

The man he now knew to be Larry, Chelsea's brother, was at the stove, stirring a large pot of sauce and singing an obscure aria. His wife, the redheaded nurse, was laughing at the antics of a toddler she was trying to feed. And at the center table, two young people were putting together a salad, much of which was flying through the air as they tossed it at each other, squealing and ducking.

Chelsea cleared her throat. The two young people continued to throw lettuce, but Larry turned. The aria ended, his back straightened, and behind those scholarly glasses his eyes filled with something black and fierce.

Mimi glanced up at the same time, and the humor drained from her face. "Hi," she said. Inexplicably, her restraint saddened Nick.

Finally the young people became aware of him. "Oh," the girl said, her voice dropping. Nick knew what was running through everyone's mind. What was this man doing here, this evil man who'd yelled at Chelsea and was pushing her business off Pine Ridge Mountain?

He imagined Chelsea felt the tension in the room, too. She raced through introductions, then before anyone could say anything, asked if the kids were still with the kittens. Nick felt terrible. He'd made amends with her, but he hadn't realized there was a whole family behind her who were still offended. The thought hadn't even crossed his mind, probably because he himself had never known that sort of close family loyalty.

Larry reminded Nick of a sheriff in a western movie, squint-eyes fixed, silently daring him to make a wrong move. Instead of a gun, though, he was wielding a wooden spoon dripping spaghetti sauce. Larry's displeasure bothered him more than anyone else's. He'd always regretted not having a brother, and he felt instinctively that Larry was someone he could really like.

"They're in here." Chelsea tugged Nick's shirtsleeve and took him through a short pantry.

"Cripes, how long *is* this house?"

"Deceptive, isn't it. There are four bedrooms and a bath upstairs, too."

Nick whistled softly. "Chet could've charged you four times what he did."

Chelsea felt the stirrings of anger but tamped them down. They were getting along fairly well, and she wanted to get along better—for Katie's sake.

"This leads to the barn. Mama cat insists on keeping her kittens up in the loft."

Nick's gaze roamed over the dim clutter, deciphering three wicker gondolas, various trailer beds and, in front of a double door, an old blue van painted with the same colorful logo that decorated the billboard down the road. Vague pangs of guilt pricked at his conscience again, as he tallied up the amount of junk she had to move.

"Hey! Dad!" Katie called from the top of the stairs. "Dad, come up here."

Unlike the lower level, the loft was bright with natural light pouring in the long rows of windows. It was airy, clean, the floor newly sanded. A pink wall telephone and a powerful-looking sewing machine suggested that Chelsea spent a good deal of time up here.

"C'mon, Dad." Katie waved him over to a cardboard box. Two boys who looked remarkably like Larry were sitting cross-legged on the floor near her.

"Don't touch, Katie," Nick warned softly. "Mother cats don't like people touching their babies when they're this young"

"I already touched. Chelsea let me," Katie said, sounding righteous.

Nick leaned in and gently stroked the mother's head. "You have pretty babies, Mama cat."

"She likes you." Chelsea smiled.

Just then one of the kittens got up on its spindly legs and tried to climb over a sibling. Instead, it went tumbling head over tail, sending the children into a fit of giggles. Nick and Chelsea stood back.

"Those are Larry's boys?" Nick asked.

"Yes. Matthew and Peter. I hope Katie hasn't overdone it. They've been playing hide-and-seek and doing a lot of running."

She was biting her full lower lip, and he imagined she was worrying about Grace's comment. "I'm sure she's fine." He turned around slowly, scanning the peak-roofed room. "What do you do up here?"

"Mostly repairs. For instance, the balloon stuffed in that bag has a few panels that are wearing thin. It's tedious work, taking apart all the stitching, but I save money doing it myself. And the repairs have to get done—I have an equipment inspection coming up soon."

"Oh? Is that normal procedure?"

"Of course. I get tested, too. Every year." She smirked as if she was still serving up that crow.

But Nick wasn't going to apologize for his caution. Her trophies might be proof that she was good sometimes, but sometimes she was wretched. He'd seen her fly. He'd also seen the exhilaration in her face. She got a thrill out of living on the edge.

"Katie, I hate to break this up, but we've got to go."

Katie turned reluctantly from the box, a tiny ball of fur cupped in her hands. "Can I have one, Daddy? Chelsea says she's gonna give them away. Free."

"Thanks a lot," he muttered for Chelsea's ears only. "No, Katie, not now. Maybe after we get our own place."

He felt Chelsea's attention. He looked at her and she turned away. "Were you about to say something?"

She shrugged. "I was just wondering why you won't be staying at the Lockwoods'."

They moved slowly toward the stairs. "Why would I want to do that?"

He noticed her swallow uncomfortably. "Well, it isn't a secret that you and Grace are dating. Right?"

Uncomfortable himself now, he nodded.

"And you're pretty serious."

"Where'd you hear that?"

"Grace."

Nick bristled. He felt rushed—as if Grace was presuming too much.

But she wasn't really. He'd been taking her out for more than four months. Occasionally they'd talked about the future, and he *was* considering marriage. Why, then, was he suddenly feeling claustrophobic?

"I'm sorry." Chelsea's cheeks flushed. "I didn't mean to pry. I j-just thought if you two were going to be m-married, you'd stay put at her house."

Her house. He'd never thought about it before, but of course, Grace would want to stay there.

He shook his head. He didn't want to think about that right now. "Come on, Spud. Put the kitten down."

"Can I come back tomorrow?"

Chelsea touched Nick's arm. "Katie's welcome any-time."

Her hand was a warm pressure that suddenly became the focus of all Nick's attention. He gazed into her eyes, eyes that seemed to be inviting him in, into their smoky gray warmth. "That would be..." No. What was he thinking! "I hope you don't take this wrong, but I'd rather she didn't."

The light in her eyes dimmed. Despite the brave little smile, she was hurt.

Nick dragged his fingers through his hair and sighed heavily. "It's nothing personal. I just don't want Katie around the balloon."

Chelsea nodded. "I understand."

Why did she look so disappointed? he wondered. Why should one more child mean so much to her? Nick's stomach knotted with a tension that was becoming all too familiar.

"Katie, we're going."

The kitchen was filled with steam and the aroma of bubbling spaghetti sauce as they passed through again. The two boys, who had followed them down, sidled over to the counter and reached into a bakery box. Cannoli, Nick guessed from the cream they popped into their mouths. He smiled. It would've been nice having another child. Maybe even a couple more.

"Nick?"

He shook his head. Chelsea was watching him curiously.

"Would you like to stay for dinner? We'd love to have you."

"Thank you, but we really have to go."

"Are you sure?"

Katie tugged on his belt. "Say yes, Dad!"

"You know Grace probably has dinner ready for us."

Katie only deepened his embarrassment by opening her mouth and pretending to gag. "She's making liver tonight." It didn't help that everyone else laughed.

They seemed like pretty nice people, and they certainly thought a lot of Chelsea. Nick lifted his gaze and let it touch each face. He had no idea why their opinion of him mattered, but it did. He didn't want to walk out of here with their resenting him as the Simon Legree who was turning Chelsea out of her home.

"Liver, huh? Actually, I wouldn't mind staying myself."

THE ATMOSPHERE in the dining room was restrained, but Nick refused to give up. He discussed the latest breakthroughs in physical therapy with Mimi and surprised Rob, the environmental activist, with his knowledge of issues—which grudgingly got Larry, the science teacher, involved. Minute by minute, Nick could feel the ice thawing.

By the time dessert was being passed around, he felt confident enough to bring up the touchy subject of the changes at Pine Ridge. He thought they might be interested, since they all lived in the area, and they were. Yes, Nick felt a definite thawing, and when he and Judy both reached for the last piece of pastry, his heart warmed when she battled openly, the way she would have with her sister or brother.

Occasionally, Nick glanced across the table to meet Chelsea's wide, incredulous eyes. She'd grown quiet, and he suspected she usually wasn't. He hoped he wasn't acting like a jerk and embarrassing her. He was doing an awful lot of talking and playing with the kids.

Eventually Mimi declared she couldn't look at dirty dishes one more minute. Slowly, the others rose, too. Nick was gratified that no one objected when he pitched in to help.

Nick was the last to leave. He didn't plan on it working out that way, but somehow there he was, walking Chelsea down the front hall. "Thanks for a lovely evening. Dinner was delicious."

"Glad you stayed."

Katie ran between them and out to the porch, waving goodbye to the two boys. Nick and Chelsea paused at the door.

She was awfully quiet, Nick thought. Almost peevish. Clutches of uneasiness returned. In his eagerness to get to know her family, had he slighted her? And why would she care if he had?

"I had a great time tonight," he ventured. "Your family's something else."

"Hmm, we're all pretty flaky."

"No. I think they're terrific. I like them."

She sighed resignedly. "And they apparently like you."

Feeling as if he were taking a step into space, he hooked a finger under her chin and lifted it so he could see into her eyes. "But you don't. You still don't like me, do you?"

She seemed to struggle with her answer. "And you don't like me. Why mince words?"

Nick searched her smooth, hot face, finding her features as intoxicating as champagne. "That's where you're wrong," he whispered. "I only don't *want* to like you."

Her eyes lifted to his, startled, but she was no more surprised by the comment than he. He said a hasty good-night and hurried out the door.

CHAPTER SEVEN

THE NEXT FEW DAYS passed uneventfully enough, and then calamity struck. Chelsea had been looking at rental properties all morning, her poor old van coughing and wheezing from one hill to the next, when suddenly, shifting became quite difficult. She was accustomed to the engine's sickly noises, but this stiffness in the gears was something new.

She'd headed back toward town immediately and had almost made it, but she'd had to be towed the last two miles.

Now Chelsea eased herself onto the wall outside the gas station and lowered her head into her hands. She was tired beyond exhaustion and recognized it for what it was—depression.

Buck, the mechanic she always came to with her problems, was checking the van now. With any luck, he'd ply his usual magic and she'd be rolling again, tomorrow at the latest.

But Chelsea strongly suspected her luck was running out. She hadn't had any looking at houses this morning, she still had to find a way to move her billboard, and the van was living on borrowed time.

She swung her feet up onto the wall and leaned her back against the sun-warmed brick of the garage. Why now? she asked, fighting an urge to cry.

She closed her eyes and immediately an image of Nick Tanner took form. Damn him! He was the cause of every misery in her life, the most irritating of which was the fact that he was on her mind constantly these days. No amount of work or worry could drive him out. When she least expected it, she'd find herself remembering things—the easy way he'd traded jokes with Rob at dinner the other night, his absorption in teaching baby Beth to play pat-a-cake.

Before he'd arrived, Chelsea had asked her family to be civil, but the degree to which they'd gotten along with him surpassed her wildest expectations. Then it occurred to her that Nick was a businessman. He was used to charming people. By now it was probably second nature, this winning friends, influencing people. That was undoubtedly it. She'd hate to think he was really as charming as he appeared.

The only problem was, if it was all an act, she couldn't come up with a reason for it. What could he possibly gain by ingratiating himself with her family? And ingratiate himself he had. She'd wanted them to be civil but, Lord, they'd practically sat up and begged. They'd made him the center of attention, him and his harebrained vision of Pine Ridge. They'd even forgotten that that vision was precisely the reason her life was now in a state of upheaval.

Chelsea tried to enjoy the sunshine warming her face. Forget him, she told herself. Most likely, he'd never be back. He'd made it clear he didn't want Katie at the house, didn't want her thinking about balloons. Forget him, she repeated as the sun soaked into her tired muscles.

But she couldn't, because the honest truth was he had charmed her right along with her family. Not that she thought he'd meant to; the man had barely spoken to her all evening. But she *was* charmed. Listening to his warm, impassioned voice as he spoke about Pine Ridge, watching his expressive hazel eyes, his beautifully shaped mouth... Before long she had felt positively inebriated.

There was also that conversation at the door. She couldn't even think about that moment without grinning ear to ear.

Nick liked her. He'd admitted that, though he was fighting it, he *liked* her.

Of course, it meant nothing to her personally. The man was going with Grace Lockwood. But it was still wonderful news—for Katie. Maybe there was hope for a balloon ride yet.

Grace. Chelsea's eyelids squeezed in a wince. She didn't know why the thought of Nick's dating Grace bothered her so. Grace was attractive, intelligent and a wonderful home-maker. But she did have an edge that grated. She could be humorless, rigid—an old futz! Chelsea knew that love was blind, but something about this match seemed extraordinarily wrong.

"That all you do all day, Lawton?"

Chelsea snapped open her eyes. "Nick!" She sat up straight, her heart immediately racing.

His car was at a gas pump, and he was standing beside the open door. His eyes were warm with humor. In that instant Chelsea realized she wasn't so much upset by the fact that he was dating Grace as by the fact that he was dating anyone at all.

He unscrewed his gas cap and reached for the pump. "What are you doing here?"

Chelsea watched the play of muscles beneath his cream-colored shirt. He must work out, she decided. He certainly wasn't bulky, but his shoulders were broad, his arms strong and corded. She jerked her thumb toward the open bay of the garage. "My van."

"What's wrong with it?"

"Don't know yet." Her gaze traveled the length of him. She didn't know why he continued to interest her. To be honest, she'd dated a couple of guys with better builds and one who was actually better looking. Still, Chelsea knew no one had ever touched that part of her deep inside that was primal and female and beyond all reasoning. Not the way Nick Tanner did.

She frowned, furious with herself. She had no right to think about him this way. The man was taken. Besides, he was the enemy! He was ruining her life.

Lecturing herself didn't seem to make any difference, though. Her heart, or hormones—whatever was responding to Nick—had a mind all its own.

He finished pumping, paid his bill, then walked toward her. If her pulse had been beating fast before, it now raced out of control.

"Hi," he said, sitting beside her. "Mind if I join you?"

"It's a free wall. Lunch break?"

He nodded, his eyes never leaving her face. She wondered if he saw any of the ravages of her morning written there. She hoped not. The Fates might be dumping all over her, but that was her business. There was no need for him to gloat.

"How goes the house hunt these days?"

"The . . . How'd you know?"

"Know what?"

"That I . . . Never mind. It's going. And with you?"

Nick was about to answer when Buck stepped out of the garage, wiping his hands on a grease-blackened rag. Chelsea jumped to her feet, alert and praying for good news with every fiber of her being. She couldn't afford to have the van off the road right now, and she couldn't afford another bill.

Buck shook his shaggy gray head. "You want to hear it now or later?"

She wrung the ribbing of her sweater. "How bad?"

"Bad. Your transmission's shot."

She expelled her breath as if she'd been punched. "Are you sure?"

"Wish I could say no."

"How much to fix it?"

"Sure you want to bother? That van of yours is in here every other month. I have a beauty of a Dodge in the back you might want to consider instead."

Chelsea glanced toward the wall, but Nick had thoughtfully removed himself and was pacing a respectful distance away.

"Fixing the van has to be cheaper than buying something new."

"At this point it's throwing good money after bad."

"Buck!" She didn't want to plead. "Maybe in a few months. Not now. How much will the transmission be?"

He sighed, then told her. Chelsea wished she were the fainting sort. Fainting would be so much better than standing here shaking.

"You okay, kid?"

"Yes. Fine." She squared her shoulders. "How long?"

"A couple days."

"Then do it."

"If you say so. Do you have a way to get home?"

Chelsea rubbed her hands over her face, hoping to give the impression she was thinking. Actually, she'd felt moisture gathering in her eyes and wanted to swipe it away.

"I can give her a lift."

Buck looked over at Nick. "That okay with you, Chelsea?"

She nodded. The mechanic waved and headed back to work.

"I hate putting you out, Nick, but I do appreciate the favor," she said, slipping into his Volvo.

"My pleasure."

As the car hummed along, Chelsea closed her eyes, glad that Nick didn't insist on talking. She'd have to do some serious thinking about her life-style when she got home—about finding another job, about living with roommates. It wasn't a scenario she'd pictured for herself at her age. She'd hoped for more solidity and permanence, but she supposed compromise was what growing up was all about.

When she opened her eyes again, they'd reached Pine Ridge Road, but as they neared her house, she noticed Nick wasn't slowing down. "Hey!" She pointed, as the house sailed by. But he kept on going, chewing on a small mischievous smile. "Nick! Where are you going?"

"Lunch. Feel like joining me?"

"This isn't necessary," Chelsea sat stiff in her seat as they turned onto the highway. "What are you *doing!*"

He flashed her a heart-stopping smile. "The truth? You look as if you could use a break."

Chelsea hardened herself against a quivering in her jaw. She didn't expect this kindness from him. "Where are you taking me?"

"Frankly, I'm not really sure...how about we go exploring and see what turns up? Since moving here, I haven't had much time to look around. This'll be a break for me, too." Nick leaned forward to read a passing sign. "Hmm. Stockbridge. That sounds good. Always wanted to visit Stockbridge."

"You mean you've never been there? Ever?"

"It doesn't make me a bad person, Chelse."

She bit back a smile. She kind of liked this new, easygoing side to Nick Tanner and she loved the effortless way he'd called her Chelse, as if the more intimate nickname was already a part of his vocabulary. "Stockbridge is lovely. You'll think you've walked into a Norman Rockwell painting. He lived there much of his life, you know."

A few minutes later, they were driving up the town's wide main street. It was only May, but the shops were already busy with tourists.

"This looks interesting." Nick surprised her by swerving abruptly into a parking spot.

She retrieved her purse, which had slid to the floor, and gazed up at the mammoth white inn, its porch bright with geraniums. "Interesting? Nick, this is the Red Lion Inn."

"Oh, I've heard of that. Pretty classy place. Great. Let's have lunch here."

She gulped.

"My treat."

"I'm not dressed right."

Nick flicked his tie. "I'll cover for both of us."

They had a perfectly wonderful meal that lasted an hour and a half. Whenever conversation threatened to get too serious, Nick signaled a time-out and steered them clear. By the time dessert arrived, Chelsea felt much better. She swallowed a spoonful of strawberry parfait and sighed with contentment.

"By the way, where's Katie?"

Nick stirred his coffee. He'd passed up dessert but seemed to be getting a kick out of watching Chelsea eat hers. "With Grace. Grace has started to tutor her. It's working out remarkably well."

Chelsea poked valleys into her dessert with her spoon. She'd thought Katie was a safe subject. "That's good."

There was an uneasy pause. "What's the matter?"

"Nothing."

"Yes, there is. Your voice has this irritating little edge to it."

"Thanks a lot." She tried to smile but failed.

"You're welcome. And I mean it."

Chelsea moved aside her half-eaten parfait. "Okay, maybe something is wrong. Maybe it bothers me that Katie's not going to a regular school."

Nick leaned back and huffed a long sigh. "I thought so."

"Sorry, it's none of my business, of course...."

"No, don't apologize. I've been round that same mulberry bush myself a few dozen times, but I think I'm mak-

ing the right decision. You have to understand, Katie's
education so far has been terribly fractured. She's missed a
lot of school because of her operations. She should be in
second grade now, but this year she's repeating first."

"Oh. I didn't realize that." Chelsea felt a heartache she
couldn't have anticipated. "But it's certainly understandable after all she's been through."

"You don't know the half of it, Chelse." Pain filled his
eyes. "Tutors seem to work well. Katie had one back in
Boston who helped a lot, and Grace is a certified teacher."

"Yes, I know."

"I've talked to the principal at the local school here. He
has some standardized tests we can measure her progress by,
and if she scores well, he says there should be no problem
giving her grade credit."

Chelsea had to admit it made sense. "So, next September she'll be going into the second grade at the local
school?"

"No. I'm going to have Grace tutor her for a few years.
Home education's exactly what someone in Katie's situation needs, the individual attention, working at her own
pace. She's a really bright kid. With individual attention
she'll catch up to grade level in no time."

Again he made sense. Chelsea didn't know why she was
disgruntled—except perhaps that she begrudged Grace's
spending so much time with Katie.

Nick studied her over the rim of his coffee cup. "You look
as if I were sentencing my daughter to a life in prison."

Chelsea made an effort to smile. "I was just thinking
about what she'll miss, that's all. Playmates and social
growth, that sort of thing."

"I'm afraid the only thing she's gained from going to
school with other kids is a whopping inferiority complex."

"Katie?"

"That's right. She's always been a few steps behind everyone else, academically, emotionally and, of course, physically."

"But she's almost better."

"She's never going to be better, Chelsea," Nick replied with a bitterness she hadn't seen before. "Not a hundred percent."

"So, what are you going to do, keep her isolated the rest of her life?"

"She'll have lots of opportunity to meet other kids."

"Nick, I know it's none of my business, but have you ever considered the possibility that you're being a bit too protective of Katie? Maybe she needed that treatment once, but she's ready to move on."

"Dammit, Chelse! You think I don't want her to move on? You think I don't want the best for her? But let's face facts. She's . . ."

"Handicapped?"

Nick was breathing heavily now. "I love Katie," he said with a conviction so deep his voice shook, "and it tears me up when I think about all the things she'll miss out on, the normal things other girls will take for granted. Dancing, becoming a cheerleader—dumb little stuff like that."

"As far as I can see, the only handicap she has right now is you."

Nick reared back, stunned. Remorse gripped her immediately.

"I'm sorry. I had no right to say that. It's just that I hate to see her being treated like an invalid. I can't help thinking she'd be better off if everybody forgot her past and let her get on with her life."

Nick shook his head sadly. "I can't forget. Neither would you if you'd been forced to live through it. And I see nothing wrong with protecting her. I'm her father. That's what I'm here for."

Chelsea opened her mouth to argue, but just one look into his face changed her mind. After years of dealing with parents and kids from the hospital, she knew pain, and Nick's ran deep. "Nick, let's not argue. This..." She encompassed the elegantly set table, the room—and him. "This has been too nice. I don't want to spoil it."

"I didn't mean to."

She smiled tentatively, but he didn't smile back.

Out on the sidewalk Nick took her arm when she started for the car. "Wait. Let's take a walk. I don't feel like going back just yet. Do you?"

Chelsea shook her head. Maybe a walk would dissipate the tension that had fallen over their good mood.

They spent nearly an hour wandering through shops. Nick's favorite was a general store complete with potbellied stove and floorboards that squeaked.

"What can we do next?" he asked as they headed back up the sidewalk. His spirits had recovered completely, it seemed. Chelsea had to laugh. "Humor me, Chelse. I've been stuck in a thirty-story bank the last ten years."

"Okay. How about the Rockwell Museum?"

Nick considered. "Nah, it's too nice a day. Some other time."

They walked leisurely, their hands in their pockets. Every so often their arms bumped in companionable warmth.

"I know," Chelsea announced when they reached the car. "Ever been to Bash Bish Falls?"

"Bash what? I can't even say it."

"Let's go then. I'll give you directions."

They headed south, Nick attacking the steep hills and curves with an enthusiasm that gladdened Chelsea's heart. Though she'd lived here all her life, she, too, found the ride immensely enjoyable.

"Bash Bish Reservation," she read off a sign. "Turn here." They parked in a designated area, then headed up a woodland path.

"Did Larry tell you we ran into each other last night?"

"No. I haven't talked to him today," she replied.

"Hmm. At the drugstore." Nick gazed ahead at the rising path. A brook tumbled by on their right. The air was fresh and sweet with new life. "While we were talking he explained what was going on that day you strafed the ski area in your balloon."

Chelsea felt a warm surge of vindication.

"I'm sorry about the misconception I had of you. Larry told me all about the kid, about how you were only trying to teach him a lesson."

"Yeah, well, people who disregard the rules of ballooning don't sit very high in my estimation. No matter what you think, I'm one of the most careful balloonists you'll ever meet, Nick. That's one virtue my grandfather insisted on drumming into me. He told me horror stories, made me read diaries..."

"He sounded like a fascinating man, the little you got to say about him at the Lockwoods."

"He came into my life at exactly the right time."

"Hmm. Your father had just died?"

"That's right. My grandfather helped a lot. He and I got to be real pals. We shared this love that nobody else really understood."

"Ballooning."

"Yes. I don't expect you to understand. You'd have to experience it personally."

"Which isn't very likely."

Chelsea groaned. "Ballooning really is safe, you know, and I'm good at it. Not that I give a hoot whether or not you ever take a ride, but it's an experience you wouldn't want to miss. Almost mystical. Stop laughing." She swatted his arm.

"Speaking of mystical..." Nick stood transfixed, glimpsing the slender waterfall she'd brought him to see. It rushed from a stony gorge above and plunged a dramatic fifty feet into a clear, rock-bottomed pool.

They found a spot off the path where they could sit, and for a long while watched the falls without speaking. Chelsea felt close to Nick, as if she knew him better than she did. There was nothing about their brief acquaintance that warranted the feeling, but still she couldn't shake it.

"There's a legend that goes with these falls." Her voice softened. "According to the story, there once was an Indian maiden who was so saddened by unrequited love that she leapt to her death from that ledge up there. Some people say her spirit haunts the falls, and if you listen real hard to the rushing of the water, you can still hear her crying."

She smiled self-consciously. The story was common treacle. But as the seconds spun out, and even their breathing quieted, she realized they were both listening, hard. Aware of what they were doing, they laughed.

Overhead, a warm breeze flicked the small new leaves of the trees. Birds were making a May racket. Chelsea felt the closeness return, and suddenly she had the strangest urge to share things with Nick.

"Nick?" Her voice sounded small and unsure.

"Mmm." He raised a knee and rested his chin on it.

"About my ballooning... It's safe, but I have had a few close calls in my time."

He turned his head, his gaze narrowing.

"I've had scrapes...accidents. We have these things in the mountains called rotors, sort of like little whirlwinds, and I got caught in one once." She paused. "I don't know why

I'm telling you this. You already have a warped enough idea . . ."

"No. Go on."

She shrugged. "It was the most terrifying experience of my life. I remember thinking, 'This is it. This is the time and place I'm going to die.'"

Nick lifted his hand to her shoulder protectively. "But obviously you didn't. What happened?"

"I don't know. Oh, I know what I did, but I don't know how or why—my mind was in such a panic. All I know is that suddenly I was firing up the burner, and the balloon began to rise. I was hanging on for dear life. The basket was spinning out . . . I heard a tear. But all at once I was out of it. I'd risen right out of it!" Her voice lifted with amazement.

Beside her, Nick expelled his breath in a quick release. His hand moved from her shoulder across her back. "Maybe your grandfather was on the ride with you."

"Maybe so." She followed the sunlight playing over his face, over the deep brown silk of his hair. He noticed her watching him and abruptly dropped his hand.

Chelsea felt confused. She'd told herself the hand on her shoulder was merely a gesture of comfort, but no amount of rationalizing could minimize the electricity that had just sparked between them.

She made an effort to clear her mind. "Nick?"

"Yes?"

"I guess I told you that story so you'd realize I've experienced the worst there is, and the sheer terror has made me cautious to the point where I'll never risk having those experiences again. I treasure my life and the lives of everyone I take up."

Nick gazed ahead, frowning. His eyes looked lost, wistful, and Chelsea wondered what could possibly be on his mind.

"We'd better be heading back." Nick tossed a swift evasive smile in her direction. "It's after four."

She sighed, reluctant to end their afternoon, but she knew it was time. Nick had pulled into himself, and there would be no opening that door again today.

CHAPTER EIGHT

THE NEXT EVENING, Chelsea got a call from Larry. Earlier in the day he'd placed an order for a balloon of his own and was beside himself with excitement.

"One more thing, sis. Someone just called me to charter a flight, and I wanted to know if tomorrow would be okay."

Chelsea wondered why this person had called Larry and not her. Perhaps it was a friend of his from school. "Sure. The weather's supposed to be great. Are you free to crew, or should I ask one of my students?"

"Actually, I was wondering if I might take the flight myself."

"Oh. Oh, well, sure." When Larry had gotten his license, Chelsea had discussed sharing piloting duties with him occasionally and had worked out terms. "Do you want me to crew for you?"

"That depends."

"On what?"

"On whether you want to, after I tell you who I'm taking up."

"Who, for heaven's sake?"

"Nick Tanner."

The news hit Chelsea like a blow to the solar plexus. "Nick agreed to ride in a balloon?"

"Not agreed. Asked."

"I don't believe it!"

"Surprised me, too."

"Is Katie going?"

"No. And he made me promise she'd never find out he went without her. I guess the kid's been bugging him about it."

"Hmm. Why did he call you?" Chelsea asked.

"I don't know."

"Maybe he feels more confident flying with a man."

"Or maybe he finds it easier to eat humble pie with me."

Larry was probably right. Still, it hurt.

"I get the feeling Nick would prefer you didn't even find out about this flight," Larry added.

"I'm sure that's true, but I do know, and what's more, I'm going to help crew."

Chelsea hung up the phone and slumped in her office chair, then began rocking in a steady, nervous rhythm. Ten minutes later she picked up the receiver and called her brother back.

"Larry, I have a favor to ask. I've been promising the little Leandro girl a ride for weeks. I can't put it off much longer. Would you mind if she went along with Nick?"

"No. Of course not."

"Good. Now for the second half of my favor. Do you mind if I take your place? I'll pay you your usual fee for booking a flight *and* for piloting."

"You're the boss," he finally conceded.

EIGHT-YEAR-OLD Heather Leandro and her mother arrived at the field before Nick. The air was mild on this late afternoon, but Heather was dressed warmly, with sturdy shoes and pants and a jacket with the hood tied up around her eager face. She was a veteran of ballooning, a familiar sailor of the skies.

When Nick arrived, she was pulling at the folds of the balloon spread out across the field, while Chelsea aimed two large fans into the opening at the bottom. The nylon was starting to billow and fill.

Nick got out of his car wearing a rueful smile. "Somehow I had a feeling you'd be here, Lawton. You couldn't let me sneak even one quick flight behind your back, could you?"

Chelsea waved and smiled.

"Say, Nick." Larry came forward and the two shook hands. The whir of the fans drowned out most of their conversation, but from the sharp glance Nick cast in Chelsea's direction, she surmised that Larry was telling him he wouldn't be piloting today.

"It's going to be a beautiful evening for a ride," Chelsea called. "Perfect for your first time. The air's so calm, visibility endless . . ."

He strode over. "This isn't what I arranged. I chartered a solo flight. I thought I'd be alone."

"You didn't count on me, either, did you?"

Heather skipped forward, her dark brown eyes fastened on Nick. She flashed him an irresistible smile. "Don't be afraid, mister. I've been up plenty of times. It's great!"

Nick groaned—and then laughed, apparently accepting his plight. "Anything I can do to help?"

"That's the spirit." Chelsea winked.

When the balloon was almost ready, she called to Heather's mother, a young, attractive brunette leaning against her car. "Feel like coming along, Jan?"

"Are you sure?" Jan knew how expensive a ride normally was.

"Sure, I'm sure."

"Hi, I'm Jan Leandro, Heather's mother," she said, climbing in.

"Nick Tanner," he responded.

"Okay, here we go." Chelsea unclipped the tether line and tossed it to Larry. She turned up the burner, and a long, hot blast leapt into the nylon bubble. Heather giggled with anticipation. The basket rocked, then up it went, lightly, gently, easy as a cloud.

Nick's fingers were white, gripping the lines overhead. His eyes were wide and he seemed to have stopped breathing.

"It's going to be fine," Chelsea whispered in his ear.

The earth dropped away and soon they were drifting, ever so slowly, over the field ripe with wild daisies and yellow buttercups. With every passing second, the perspective changed, opened out. Far below, Larry was already in the Jeep, trailing the balloon.

Heather kneeled on a small corner bench, arms on the rail cushioning her chin. She was having a grand time, singing some song she'd learned in school. Her mother, standing beside her, smiled as she caught Chelsea's eye.

Soon they were gliding over the ski area, high enough for all the Berkshires to be spread out below them. Chelsea noticed Nick wasn't holding on so tightly anymore, and his face had relaxed. Then he spoke so softly she almost didn't hear him. "This is wonderful."

Chelsea was sure something inside her melted. "Think so?"

He smiled and nodded, his glittering hazel eyes filled with the majesty of the view. "It feels weird—like we're standing still and the earth is what's moving by. I never expected this . . . this stillness. Or this silence."

"Lots of first-time passengers say that," Chelsea assured him. "One even confessed to feeling he was traveling in another dimension." Chelsea knew what each of them meant, no matter how they phrased it. "I suppose that feeling comes from the fact that we're moving with the air, not faster, not slower. That's why it's so still, why there's no sound or sensation of movement."

"Tell him to light a match, Chelsea," Heather's small, knowing voice piped up.

"Good idea." Chelsea found the book she always carried in her sweatshirt pocket. "Go on, strike a match."

Nick did, and the flame burned without a flicker. "Well, I'll be!" He stared at it till it nearly burned his fingers.

"I wish I'd brought a camera," he said a little while later. "This view takes your breath away."

"Don't you feel like a bird?" Heather exclaimed.

"Like an eagle, at least." Nick smiled warmly at the child. "How old is she?" he asked Mrs. Leandro.

"Eight."

"Ah." He nodded. "I have a daughter, too. She's seven, going on thirty."

Mrs. Leandro laughed. "I know what you mean."

Chelsea was thrilled that Nick was enjoying himself. Until this moment, she hadn't known how very much she'd wanted him to.

"Okay, Heather, how many mountains can you name?" Chelsea challenged.

"That's easy. There's October Mountain, and that's Mount Wilcox, the one with the pink cloud almost on it. And way out there," she pointed, "is Mount Greylock."

"She's awfully bright," Nick commented. "My knowledge of these mountains begins and ends with Pine Ridge."

Mrs. Leandro looped her arm around her daughter and gave her an affectionate hug.

"The light's positively unearthly this evening, isn't it?" Chelsea commented. The entire world seemed awash in shades of rose and gold. "Okay, Heather, let's make a run for the river."

"Awright!" the child cheered.

Chelsea pulled on the line that vented the hot air, and slowly they slid earthward. She picked up the radio. "Larry, we're dropping in on the Housatonic for a while."

"Roger. Have fun. Wish I were with you."

The Housatonic River rushed and tumbled over its stony bed, sparkling with the slanting rays of the westering sun. By venting carefully, Chelsea brought the basket down until it just skimmed the water. The woods rose up on either side like walls of a leafy canyon. Ahead of them, a fish leapt into the air, and for one split second became a part of the ethereal light. Chelsea heard Nick's quick intake of breath and felt his excitement as her own. Sharing this experience, seeing him enjoy what she loved most in life, pleased her more than she had ever anticipated.

At a bend in the river, she took them over the treetops again, and from there up and over a ridge into a different valley. They'd just lost touch with their chase vehicle, but she wouldn't alert Nick to that fact. Besides, Larry would catch up—eventually.

The valley was as picturesque as the Berkshires got, but when Chelsea happened to glance at Nick, she was startled to find him watching her instead of the scenery. A smile warmed his eyes, softened his mouth. Suddenly she found breathing almost impossible. Good heavens, but the man made her dizzy! With an effort she looked away.

The shakiness stayed with her, however. It was preposterous that Nick should affect her this way, but she was becoming used to the fact that reason wasn't controlling her reactions. She also knew she'd arranged this flight purposely, not merely to accommodate Heather, but because she'd wanted to be the one Nick shared his first balloon flight with. She'd sold her brother the story about Heather because, if she was really honest, it was a good excuse to be with Nick again. Her behavior wasn't just preposterous, it was reprehensible.

The radio crackled. "Ground to Chelsea. Do you read me?"

"Hi, Larry. You found us!" The guy was a gem. "Where are you?"

They established location, and Larry added, "I hate to pull the plug on you, but the sun's dipping behind the ridge."

"I know." It wouldn't do to be caught in the boondocks without light. It'd happened before, fortunately without passengers, and she'd had to come down into trees. Not an experience she ever wanted to repeat. "There's a farm ahead, though I'm not sure whose it is."

"I'll run ahead and find out," Larry said.

A short time later he confirmed that he'd cleared a landing with the property owner.

"How was it?" Larry asked as Nick hoisted himself out of the basket.

Nick made a thumbs-up motion and grinned. Chelsea couldn't wipe the smile off her own face, either.

She ran to the Jeep and dug out a bottle of champagne for the farmer and his family who stood by, excited to near wordlessness at having such a marvelous event occur in their field. Then she opened a bottle for her passengers.

Nick lifted an eyebrow. "What's this?"

"Tradition." Crickets were singing in the deepening shadows now. Peace stilled the air. He held her gaze as he took the glass from her. "Thank you," he whispered. She knew his gratitude wasn't only for the champagne.

Heat pooled in Chelsea's cheeks. She'd never been so aware of a man in her life—of the scent of him, the texture of his skin, his breathing, eyes, lips, his laugh, his walk. She had to shake off this obsession.

She turned and poured out sparkling cider for Heather. "Here you go, mademoiselle."

"Oh, thank you." Before taking the glass, however, Heather unzipped her windbreaker and untied her hood. When she did, the hood fell back, exposing her head.

Chelsea saw Nick's eyes narrow and awareness jolt through him. He looked away quickly and drained his glass.

His face had become a mask, but not fast enough. Chelsea had already seen his pained shock.

"We didn't make a toast," Heather chided him.

Nick slapped his forehead. "How rude of me."

Chelsea was amazed at how quickly he'd caught his balance. No one else had even noticed him totter. She refilled his glass and watched him clink it to the child's.

"To...balloon rides...and soft May nights...and beautiful ladies to share them with," he said.

The return to Pine Ridge was jovial, filled with chatter of the flight, but when they were back at the field and everyone but Nick and Chelsea had gone, he finally unloaded the question on her.

"What's the matter with Heather?" He kept his eyes trained on the Jeep's windshield.

"Cancer." All the magic drained out of the night.

"I figured that much. What kind?"

"Bone. A rare form." After too long a silence, she gathered the courage to look at him. His jaw was set in an angry thrust, yet his eyes seemed lost in sorrow. "She's in remission right now."

"But? I hear a 'but' in your voice."

"Chances are it'll recur within the year." A sadness she'd suppressed all evening now consumed her.

Nick let loose a harsh string of curses, and when he'd finished, he slumped against the door like an exhausted boxer retiring to his corner, quietly watching the moon rise over Pine Ridge Mountain. Its pale white light deepened all the sad lines of his face. "That poor little girl."

"Nick, I'm sorry. Maybe I should have warned you...."

He didn't appear to be listening.

"We should go," she decided. "We're not doing anyone any good sitting..."

Suddenly she felt a change, a slow, hot force rising inside Nick that scared her. He stiffened, straightened, then slowly turned.

"What did you think you were doing, Chelsea?" The ice in his voice startled her.

"Wh-what?"

"I don't like playing games."

"And I don't understand," she said, her voice rising in fear and frustration. Why was he so angry? And why at her?

"Don't play stupid, Chelsea. You set me up, and you know it. What did you expect to accomplish? Did you want to open my eyes? Teach me a lesson? You have a thing about teaching people lessons, don't you? Well, somebody ought to fill you in—it isn't attractive. It's superior and holier-than-thou, and on top of that, how I feel about my daughter is none of your damn business!"

Chelsea fell back against the seat, flabbergasted. What was he accusing her of? What, dear Lord, had she done? "I wish you'd explain. What's got you so upset?"

His answer was a sharp, disdainful laugh. "You're unbelievable! Simply unbelievable!" He shook his head in thorough disgust. "I'm going home."

Somehow that hurt most of all, his refusal to oblige her with even an explanation. He left the Jeep and walked to his car, moving as if he couldn't stand her company even one more second.

And then Chelsea was sitting alone, awash in tears and moonlight in the middle of her empty field.

CHAPTER NINE

EVERY MORNING for the next week, Nick woke up hoping he'd feel better about the evening he'd gone ballooning. But he never did. Whenever he thought about Heather Leandro, his gut knotted with anger and sorrow. How could life be so indiscriminating in its cruelty?

Damn that Chelsea Lawton and her meddlesome ways! She had no right playing games with people's emotions. Who did she think she was, anyway? Hadn't she anticipated how torn up he'd feel?

But of course she had. That was her whole point. She'd wanted him to meet a child who was truly ill. She'd wanted to shock him into realizing how healthy Katie was in comparison, to ram a sense of thankfulness down his throat. She'd probably gotten a kick out of it, too.

How he hated being manipulated! He wanted to take Chelsea by the shoulders and shake her senseless—or at least tell her off—and several times during that long week he caught himself with his hand on the phone, ready to dial her number. At the last minute, though, something always pulled him back.

He was relieved so much was going on at Pine Ridge these days. The engineering crew had arrived to mark out the new trails, and the architect had finally submitted satisfactory plans for the base village. The old buildings were being renovated, too, and Nick leapt at the opportunity to burn off his frustrations with hammer and saw. Now, if only physical exertion could help him forget how stricken Chelsea had looked, he'd be fine.

But he couldn't. Right in the middle of a job, up on a roof replacing shingles, Nick would find himself recalling her startled gray eyes when he'd turned on her, the confusion in her voice, the sheen of tears. Either she was a very good actress, or...

No. Nick couldn't accept the fact that Chelsea was as guileless as she looked or that his being thrown together with a child with terminal cancer was merely a coincidence. Yet, as the week passed and his uneasiness continued, Nick wondered if he wasn't the one who had made the mistake.

Oddly, he longed more than ever to be living on his own, and he doubled his efforts to locate an apartment. He knew he should be thankful to have the Lockwood home open to him, but the truth was, he couldn't stand staying there anymore. It was the formality of the house. It was having to spend the evening with the man he'd worked side by side with all that day. Sure, that was it.

But when Nick faced himself in the mirror after a restless night of dreaming about Chelsea, he knew there was more to his discontent than that. His only consolation was that he recognized the absurdity of the attraction. Chelsea was everything he didn't want in a woman. He would just keep his distance until the fascination passed. And it would. Nothing like that ever lasted.

In the meantime, the thing he had to do was pay more attention to Grace. So he watched TV with her one evening. They played cards on another. But by Saturday, when they could've spent the entire day together, he took Katie shopping instead.

She needed summer clothes, and this was a perfect time to shop, before everything got picked over. Grace offered to come along, but as tactfully as possible Nick declined. He enjoyed his time alone with Katie. She was growing too fast, and he feared it wouldn't be long before she wouldn't want to shop with him at all.

They were strolling through a mall in Pittsfield when thoughts of Chelsea returned to haunt him. There was no reason it happened there and then; Katie was chattering on about the virtues of pistachio ice cream, and he was trying not to drop any of their purchases, when suddenly he heard Chelsea's voice swirling through his busy brain. *I wish you'd explain. What's got you so upset?*

He shook his head, but the voice was only replaced by a vision of her tear-bright eyes, her small, full mouth trying to be so brave. Perhaps he'd jumped to conclusions. Perhaps she wasn't the schemer he figured her to be, after all.

He resumed a purposeful stride. He should take Grace out tonight, to dinner or the movies. She'd like that. They hadn't been anywhere in ages.

"Dad, I have to go to the bathroom," Katie interrupted. They were outside the mall washrooms.

"Sure. Can you manage by yourself?"

"Dad! What do you think I am? A baby?"

Nick smiled. "Of course not"

Handicapped? Chelsea's voice taunted him. He leaned against the wall of the adjacent store, feeling exhausted. Maybe he did coddle Katie too much, but so what?

As if she were a devil on his shoulder, Chelsea whispered back, *She needs to get on with her life.*

Nick turned aside as if trying to avoid a real physical presence and concentrated on a display window instead. The window belonged to a jewelry store. Good, he thought. Maybe he should start looking for a ring for Grace.

There were no engagement rings in this particular display, however, only hand-tooled silver—earrings, belts, necklaces. One-of-a-kind, slightly left-of-center items like the things Chelsea usually wore. Damn! he swore, swinging away. She had no right invading his life like this. No right at all.

GRACE THOUGHT a movie was a wonderful idea. A Disney classic was being rerun at the local theater, and she assured Nick it was a movie they'd enjoy as much as Katie.

The three of them were just getting out of Nick's car when a red Corvette pulled into the adjacent parking slot.

"Oh, look. It's Chelsea!" Katie exclaimed, running over.

After a week of thinking about Chelsea, Nick was ready to believe he really and truly was haunted. Slowly he let his gaze lift over the hood of his car to meet hers. She looked just as awkward as he felt.

Grace evidently knew the gallumphing adolescent Chelsea was with. She introduced him to Nick as Ted McGillis.

"Which movie are you going to?" Ted asked. Nick didn't know why he disliked Ted. He'd never even met him before.

"The cartoon," Katie answered.

Ted replied, "Hey, us, too."

They'd have to sit in the same theater? Nick's heart plummeted. His eyes linked with Chelsea's again, just for a second before she glanced away. She looked tired and upset, as if she'd had a bad week. Nick's insides twisted.

"Chelsea, I want to thank you for having Nickie and Katie over for dinner the other night." Grace was by Chelsea's side, walking toward the theater entrance.

"I-it was nothing."

"Oh, it was. When Nickie moved here, he didn't know anybody, and now he has so many friends. What you've done means a lot to me."

Walking behind, Nick saw Chelsea rubbing her palms along her trousers. "What I've done?"

"Yes. You introduced him to your family, and from the way Katie goes on, they obviously made her and Nickie feel very welcome. Katie loved your spaghetti sauce, too. You'll have to give me the recipe."

"Oh . . . oh, sure."

Tonight Chelsea was wearing ordinary navy trousers and a white silk shirt, but in her inimitable fashion she'd tied a colorful scarf around her shoulders, which rendered the outfit anything but ordinary. He watched the blouse shimmer under the parking-lot lights...watched the sweet, light sway of her hips. Maybe it wasn't so much the scarf, he thought . . .

Grace was still going on—about what? he wondered distractedly.

"I was so afraid he wouldn't like living here, and maybe, well, we'd have to move." Grace's voice lowered but not enough to escape Nick's hearing. He tensed, resenting the assumptions Grace was making.

"But now," she continued, "I think he's ready to stay and sink roots."

"I doubt it's because of anything I did, Grace."

Nick noticed how proudly Chelsea tossed her head, and he would've smiled if he didn't feel so sad, so guilty.

As luck would have it, the theater was half-empty, and they all ended up sitting together. However, Nick did manage to claim the seat at one end of their party, just as Chelsea claimed the seat at the other.

The lights dimmed and the movie began. Nick tried to lose himself in the film—he usually could—but the magic didn't work this time. He remained as aware of Chelsea as if she were up there on the screen.

About halfway through the film, he chanced a look down the row of seats, past Katie and Grace and Ted. He'd been drawn to looking toward Chelsea at least a dozen times already, but this time she returned his stare. Even in the darkness of the theater he could feel the power of her eyes, and something clutched at his breath. Suddenly he had so much he wanted to tell her: that he was a jackass for jumping to conclusions, that he shouldn't have accused her of manipulating him, that he wished she would stop being so hurt and would smile.

He didn't realize Grace was also looking at him until it was too late and she'd taken a glance at Chelsea, too. He sat back, his ears burning, and fixed his unseeing gaze on the screen. Lord, how he wished he'd brought an antacid.

When the film ended, Nick moved out into the aisle and let Katie and Grace walk ahead of him. With a feeling of delicious recklessness, he let Ted pass, too. And finally Chelsea was beside him, where he'd wanted her all along.

She tried to slip by into the crush of people crowding the aisle, but Nick found her wrist nonetheless. She froze. Her pulse beneath his fingers quickened. He leaned closer, until the intoxicating fragrance of her hair enveloped him, and whispered, "I'm sorry." Her eyes met his, startled, questioning. At that moment, they might've been the only two people in the place.

There was no time for further conversation, however. Grace had turned against the tide of exiters to search him out, her jaw clenched tight. He loosened his grip and Chelsea hurried off, carried by that tide.

ELEVEN-THIRTY, and Chelsea was sitting on the sagging sofa in her living room, sipping a mug of hot milk. She was tired. She'd asked Ted to bring her home right after the movie and had gone to bed, but she'd just lain there, wide-eyed and restless and unable to get her mind off Nick. She couldn't even shake the feeling of his fingers on her wrist.

It had been a terrible week. Nick's anger the night of their balloon flight had left her unable to sleep or eat. But tonight he'd changed. His eyes were softer, and when he'd whispered, "I'm sorry," she'd almost found herself in tears.

Did this mean he really was sorry? That he might bring Katie by again to see the kittens? And would she and Nick talk and let their newfound friendship continue to unfold?

She groaned, dropping her head into her hand. Nick Tanner was on her mind too much altogether. She had to get a grip on this situation. On this *fantasy*. She was bound to make a fool of herself if she didn't. Perhaps she already had. Grace had seemed upset tonight when she'd caught her and Nick exchanging glances. The woman wasn't blind.

But how one got a grip on a crush—and a crush was all this was—Chelsea had no idea. She'd just have to try until it wore itself out.

She was startled by a knock at her front door.

"Chelsea?"

She stood up like a shot. There was no mistaking that voice, even when it was just a raspy whisper.

She threw open the door. "Nick, what on earth . . . ?"

"Hi." His lips twitched with a strained smile.

Chelsea could barely put two coherent thoughts together. Only the one kept surfacing from her emotional turmoil: *He's here, he's here.* It pulsed through her like the beat of her heart. *He's here. He's here.*

"Oh, I'm sorry." His gaze flicked over her nightgown. "I thought you just came in. I went by a little while ago and didn't see any lights." He backed away.

"It's okay. Come in."

"It's nothing, really. I had to go up to Pine Ridge. The fire station called, but it was a false alarm, and on my way back I saw your light and figured I'd stop in for that recipe. You know, the one you and Grace were talking about?" He jammed his hands into his pockets and looked everywhere but at her.

"Come in, Nick."

He stepped into the dimly lit hall, and they both stopped again, uncertain. He was dressed as he had been earlier at the movies, in his tan trousers, white shirt and brown knit tie.

Chelsea felt an ache near to bursting in her lungs, a sensation that only increased as he raked in her appearance. She'd dashed to the door without her robe or slippers. She hadn't even run her fingers through her hair.

One corner of Nick's mouth lifted slowly. In approval? she wondered. Her long cotton gown with its yards of Victorian lace was hardly a garment to cause such a smile.

"Come into the living room and have a seat. I'll go get the recipe and be right back."

She returned within seconds, notepad and recipe in hand. "I hope nothing serious happened up at Pine Ridge..." She threw an afghan around herself before settling on the couch.

"No. Some teenagers just pulled an alarm." He sat across the room from her, at least eight feet away, but Chelsea felt a heat over her skin as if his gaze were a physical caress.

Pulling in a shuddering breath, she bent to copy the recipe.

"As long as I'm here... I'm glad I stopped by... It gives me the chance..."

She peeked up through the dark shock of hair falling over her eyes. Nick was sitting on the edge of the cushion, tapping his fingertips together. "Yes, Nick?"

He stood up, paced a few steps, then came and sat beside her, close enough that she could feel the warmth of his body, the hardness of his thigh, even through the afghan.

"I had to come over tonight, Chelse. I had to finish what I started to say in the theater. I knew I'd never get to sleep unless I did." He turned to face her more directly, bracing his arm along the back of the sofa.

"I don't want any more apologies, Nick," she whispered. "What I want is an explanation, why you were angry with me. Did you actually think I plotted to get you and Heather together to... to teach you a lesson?"

He glanced away and nodded.

"The idea never crossed my mind."

"I know. But at the time . . . just a couple of days before, we'd argued about my attitude toward Katie. I could still hear you telling me I was her biggest handicap."

Chelsea winced.

"I figured you wanted me to meet Heather to give me a sense of perspective. I got angry 'cause I thought you were trying to manipulate me. I also got angry because you dared challenge the way I was raising my daughter." He hesitated, the hard cast of his expression fading into sorrow. "But mostly I was angry because you'd made me share two hours with a wonderful little girl who probably won't see her next birthday. You'd made me get to know her and like her."

"I understand what you're saying."

"Do you?"

Chelsea gazed into his troubled eyes and nodded.

He put his arm around her shoulder and gave her a quick, tight squeeze. "I don't know how you handle it. Do you come across many kids in Heather's condition?"

"Yes, unfortunately, and I don't always 'handle' it. I've messed up quite a few times."

"How so?"

"Oh, you know . . ." Chelsea shrugged.

"No. Explain."

"Well, last summer, for instance. It was the third time this kid named Curt was flying with me. A cute little blond. Seven years old. He was in the last stages of leukemia, and I'd grown too attached, but I decided to take him up, anyway. I thought I'd been around these kids long enough not to be upset. But then he went and asked me a question that completely knocked the wind out of me.

"I remember the moment distinctly. We were drifting near Tanglewood. The evening was warm, golden, like the evening you went up, and the orchestra below was playing

The New World Symphony. We could hear the music so well, that haunting second movement. Do you know it?''

Nick nodded.

"And then, clear out of the blue, Curt looked up at me and asked if that was how he was going to feel when he was an angel.''

Nick stroked the length of her arm. "Why do you do it, Chelsea. These kids aren't your responsibility. You must lose a helluva lot of money because of them, too.''

"Beats me. Except that they give me such joy. I love helping them forget their troubles. I love seeing their eyes light up.''

Nick smiled understandingly. "Ballooning's an incredible experience. I was bowled over by it.''

"Were you really?''

"Yes." He removed his arm from her shoulder and sat forward, elbows on his knees. His smile slowly dropped until all the lines in his expression were pensive. "I have another confession to make regarding the way I blew up at you, Chelse. I didn't *want* to learn the lesson I thought you were trying to ram down my throat. I didn't *want* to accept the fact that Katie's a strong, healthy kid. As I saw it, if I continued to think she was disabled, I could go on protecting her, but if I accepted the fact that she's okay, I'd have to let go. I'd have to let her take chances, and that scares me, Chelse. It damn near terrifies me.''

"I know." Chelsea reached out and stroked his rough cheek. He leaned in to her touch, just before their eyes met. She was startled by the realization of what she was doing. She yanked her hand back and prayed he'd forget the moment.

"But scared or not," he resumed, "I have no right to put her in a cage.''

"True, but don't go overboard on me now. I've been thinking about what you said, about educating her at home, and you're right. It's exactly what she needs in order to catch up to her grade level. She'd never do it in school.''

"Yes. But I've been thinking about what you said, too, about her needing to socialize, and I'd like her back in a regular classroom as soon as she has caught up.''

Chelsea smiled. "Nice compromise, Mr. Tanner. When we put our heads together, we make a mighty impressive team." As soon as the words were out, she felt her cheeks grow hot. How forward that sounded. "H-have you reconsidered my taking her for a ride in my balloon?" she asked quickly.

Nick laughed. "I can't let go of all my hang-ups at once.''

"Does that mean you might some time in the future?''

Nick reached for her and pulled her across his body in a rough bear hug. "Will you give me a break!''

Chelsea's shriek ended in a laugh.

"Shh. You're going to wake the neighbors.''

"Serves you right. I hope they call the police,'' she said, her voice muffled against his chest.

She gripped his tie as she righted herself and, too late, heard him choking. "I'm sorry, Nick.''

"You're going to be the death of me yet.''

"Well, who in their right mind wears a tie at this time of night, anyway?'' She turned to face him more comfortably, legs tucked Indian-style, and reached for the knot. "Mind if I at least loosen it?''

"Be my guest,'' he answered, grinning. "I haven't been undressed by a woman in at least . . . well, too long.''

Her fingers fumbled and burned as they accidentally brushed the warm skin above his collar, but finally the knot slackened, and as she slowly unfastened it, her eyes lifted to his. What she saw made her heart slam against her ribs.

Whether it was his steady, smoldering gaze or the hungry curve of his mouth, she wasn't sure, but something was making her feel as if . . . as if he were pulling her into himself. And she wanted to go, to lose herself in the heady attraction. She'd never felt so drawn to a man before. No one had ever made her tremble as she was doing now.

Dear Lord! What was happening here? She pulled back, repositioned the afghan around her shoulders and retrieved the notepad that had slipped to the floor. But no amount of effort could stop her heart from racing.

Nick sat back, too, and cleared his throat. "Who was that guy you were with tonight?"

"Ted? Nice body, huh? He works at the health club." Why was she baiting him? she wondered. And why did he look so put out?

"Dating long?"

"Mmm. Since sixth grade." Nick's reaction pleased her inordinately. "Ted's a good friend. We go out occasionally as friends, but that's all."

"Oh." He seemed to be working at indifference. "How's business been?"

"Pretty good." She held the recipe toward the lamp, then bent to her scribbling again. "I ran a few newspaper ads last week. They've already paid off."

"Well, great. You should do that more often."

"Nick, I *know* what I should do. If I had the wherewithal to advertise the way I want and to buy the equipment I need, I'd double profits in no time."

Nick's gaze was like a searchlight. "Really?"

"Of course."

"Then do it. What's keeping you?"

"I told you. The wherewithal."

"Borrow it." He spoke as if walking into a loan office was as easy as whistling.

She laughed. "You're a very strange man, Nick Tanner."

"How so?"

"In your personal life, you're cautious to a fault, but when it comes to business, Chet was right, you take the wildest chances."

"They are not wild."

"Yes, they are, and that grin on your face tells me you know it, too. What's more, I think you love it."

"Well, if I'm strange, so are you, Miss Lawton. For someone who makes her living in such a risky, flamboyant way, you're mighty careful—no, fearful—when it comes to the business end of it."

Chelsea chewed on her pen, realizing he was right. But she had to be cautious. Too many loan payments, one month of bad weather, and she'd go under. The move alone was going to set her back.

Nick reached over and turned her face toward his. She shuddered with the effort to conceal her reaction.

"I hope we're not heading into another argument."

Chelsea shrugged.

"Please, let's not."

"Fine by me."

The smile he returned sent heat even to her toes. She ducked her head and continued writing.

"Oh, I found an apartment," he said.

"You did! Where?"

"Over on Pierce Road. Top floor of a duplex."

Chelsea was surprised by how pleased she was.

"It's perfect for me and Katie. Until we find a house."

"What kind of place will you be looking for—when you're ready to buy, I mean."

"Oh, I don't know. Something big. Something with substance, with a feeling of generations having lived there. Bookcases, window seats, cupboards... I have a thing about built-in nooks and odd corners. I don't know why." He thought a moment. "Maybe it's because I grew up in a two-bedroom tenement with two sisters and had to sleep on the living-room couch till I was twenty-two.''

Chelsea sat dumbstruck. Finally she just laughed.

''What's so funny?''

''I thought you were wealthy, Nick.''

''Pardon me, but I am.''

''I mean, I thought you grew up wealthy.'' She looked at him askance. ''You're putting me on. You are, aren't you?''

Chelsea loved the sound of his laugh, loved the glint of lamplight caressing his strong features.

''Afraid not, Chelse.'' His smile slowly faded.

''Was it tough, Nick?''

''Uh, no. Well, not always. Mostly it was dreary. My parents both worked in mills, one job or another, nothing ever lasting too long.''

''Are they still living?''

Nick shook his head.

''I'm sorry.'' She hated the idea of Nick's being alone in the world. ''They couldn't have been that old.''

''No, just worn out.''

''But you say you have two sisters?''

''Mmm. Cindy and Barbara. Cindy's doing okay. She married a guy from Gloucester, a lobsterman. They have two kids. Barbara, though—devil only knows where she is. She ran off when she was seventeen.''

''And you haven't seen her since?''

''No. I hired a detective, but so far... Hey, why am I telling you all this? I'm sure you don't want to hear the story of my life.''

''But I do. I had no idea. It makes what you've become that much more impressive.''

''You think I'm impressive?'' He leered comically. ''You should've seen me during my mover-and-shaker days.''

''Do you miss it? Boston?''

"No. I was ready for a change. Besides, I wanted to bring Katie here. Growing up in a city's no picnic."

"And, of course, there's Grace. This is her home."

Chelsea swore she saw Nick's face jump with a nervous tic. "Yes, of course." he said.

She sat contemplating his frown, then, hardly realizing she was speaking, she blurted, "Do you love Grace?"

His back straightened as if he'd been prodded with a cold knife. "What kind of question is that?"

She blushed furiously. "A pretty impudent one, it seems. Forget I said anything. Please."

But she couldn't forget, and neither could he.

"Grace is a wonderful woman. She's intelligent, sensible...old-fashioned, too, and I mean that in the nicest sense of the word. She enjoys keeping house. She enjoys fussing over the people in her life. I'm not a chauvinist, but I still find it charming that she cares so much about tending to a family."

Chelsea couldn't help but notice how stiff he was sitting, how little inflection was in his voice. And of course he hadn't answered her question.

"Is Grace anything like your first wife?"

"Like Laura? Hell, no! Now there was one dizzy blonde."

"I...I don't have to ask if you loved *her*."

"No," he agreed with a resigned sigh. "I loved her all right. I thought she was the most exciting thing to come down the pike."

"What was she like?" The conversation had turned more intimate than she'd ever imagined possible, yet somehow she knew it was all right."

"Hmm. What was she like? Well, she was five foot seven, blonde, blue-eyed—a real knockout, I guess you could say. You could also say she was a rebel from a well-to-do family. A sleek thoroughbred who chose to run with the pack.

She had a degree in philosophy, rode a mean little Harley and had a rose tattooed on her left cheek." He slapped his thigh so there'd be no mistaking which "cheek" he meant.

Chelsea clutched her arms, feeling increasingly inadequate, and she wasn't even in a position that warranted comparison. "Tough act to follow."

"I was awfully young when I married Laura. I'm not looking for that kind of excitement anymore. That's not the stuff marriages are made of, not lasting marriages."

Chelsea nodded as if she agreed, and she did to a point, but she couldn't help thinking that Nick was selling himself short. He didn't look particularly happy when he talked about Grace, even when he extolled her virtues, and when they were together, they didn't seem like a couple in love. They were courteous to each other, and maybe even compatible enough to pull off a peaceful marriage, but was that all Nick wanted out of life? Was it enough?

"Are you done with that?"

Chelsea glanced at the notepad and vaguely thought of adding a few more ingredients. "Uh . . . yes."

Nick took it from her and stared at it awhile. "You really ought to kick me out now." He looked up with a heart-melting grin. "Haven't I kept you up long enough?"

No! she wanted to cry. She wasn't in the least bit tired. But Nick was getting to his feet, so she did, too. The knit blanket slid to the floor, and she didn't bother to pick it up.

Nick's gaze roamed over her shoulders, down her arms, to her waifish, bare feet. "Even for bed you need someone to dress you."

A shaft of disappointment ripped through her. "What's wrong with this?" She plucked at her cotton nightgown.

"It's not any one thing. You're a whole package, Chelse." He reached out and, with a touch soft as a whisper, raised her chin. "A very nice package." Chelsea was sure her feet lifted off the floor.

They walked out to the porch where Nick paused, his brow furrowed. "Before I go..." He slid a hand into his trouser pocket and pulled out a small box embossed with the name of an expensive Pittsfield jeweler. "I went shopping with Katie today, and these happened to catch my eye." He folded Chelsea's fingers around the box. "It isn't much, just a token of my appreciation."

With hands that visibly shook, Chelsea removed the lid. Shining on a field of blue velvet was a pair of silver earrings, large hoops encircling a filigree tree. "Oh, they're beautiful, Nick." She lifted one and examined it in the pale moonlight. "But why?"

Nick shrugged his broad shoulders, slightly embarrassed. "As I said, they're a token of my appreciation. Whether you meant to or not, you did give me a new perspective on Katie. The clerk said that's a tree-of-life pattern, which I thought was kind of appropriate in this situation."

Chelsea was determined not to let the tears in her eyes spill over. She concentrated instead on putting the earrings on. Without a mirror, though, her efforts were frustrating.

"Let me." Nick took an earring in one hand, then gently brushed back her hair with the other. Holding her steady, he slipped the silver wire through the tiny pierced spot on her lobe. His touch was exquisite torture. Chelsea closed her eyes, felt her body turn fluid, as he turned her face to the other side.

"There, not bad."

Slowly, she opened her eyes, vaguely wondering why his hands were still on her neck, thumbs slowly stroking the hot skin along her jawline. Long moments passed as she gazed into his eyes and tried to gather her senses. But she couldn't. She was mesmerized by the smoky look he wore, the hunger of his mouth.

She sensed he was fighting for control, struggling with demons—and rapidly losing ground. As she was. Suddenly he pulled her into his arms with the fierceness of release, and his mouth ground down upon hers. Not a gentle kiss; he seemed to want to devour her. He groaned and whispered her name and went on kissing her, like a man too long denied.

Chelsea clung to him, weak and trembling with the fire coursing through her. From the moment they'd met, she'd known he was special. The attraction had not been imagined.

He moved his hands over her back, pressing, drawing her closer. He worked his way down to her hips, bunching the soft material of her gown in tightly clenched fists.

Chelsea arched against him with an abandon she'd never known. First kisses were not supposed to be like this, she thought. They should be gentle and shy. But this...this was madness. Wild, thrilling madness.

With a long, shivering sigh, he loosened his embrace. He shook his head, blinking his glazed eyes, as if trying to shake off a spell.

"Oh, my goodness!" Chelsea whispered as humiliation finally burned through her.

"I'm afraid goodness has nothing to do with what just happened," Nick answered. They stepped apart.

"I'm sorry, Nick."

"Don't. Don't apologize. It was my fault entirely."

"I don't know what to say." She fidgeted with the folds of her nightgown, remembering how, just a moment ago, he'd seemed about to tear it apart.

"Let's...not say anything then." His brow lowered in an angry frown. "If you don't mind, let's not say anything to anybody, okay? I'd prefer we just forget this ever happened."

She nodded, feeling her throat tighten. Okay. She got the message.

"I'd better leave now." He hadn't met her eyes for several seconds. "The earrings look nice on you. I'm glad I bought them." That said, he strode down the walk, his head jerking as if he was berating himself.

"Thank you," she finally remembered to say, but his taillights had already winked out of sight.

CHAPTER TEN

"WHY AREN'T YOU OUTSIDE, Spud?" Nick tossed his suit jacket over the couch and loosened his tie.

Katie continued to glower at the TV screen. "Grace won't let me." Nick sat down beside her. Not another incident, he prayed.

Grace appeared in the doorway, her cheeks unusually flushed. "How did your meeting at the bank go?"

"Fine." Actually, more than fine. He'd just convinced a board of stuffed shirts to cough up a few million dollars. But he didn't want to talk about bankers right now. He rose and ushered Grace into the kitchen. "Why is Katie being kept inside? It's a nice day, and she has that new bike."

Grace's eyes filled with tears. "Because she's being punished, that's why." A surprising vehemence underscored her words. "You wouldn't believe the hard time she gave me at the hospital. It was dreadful."

Just then Nick noticed the long, red scratch marks on her right arm. "Did she do that?"

Grace covered the scratches, but slowly, so that he could fully take them in. "I'm sure she didn't mean to."

"And I'm sure she did. She certainly deserves to be punished. But, Grace—" Nick clutched the nape of his suddenly aching neck "—did it have to be the bike? Couldn't you have taken away TV privileges instead?"

"I'm sorry." She lowered her eyes, her voice tremulous. "It seemed easier, that's all. When she's on her bike, I have to stop everything I'm doing to go out and watch her. You know how the traffic is on this street.''

''We don't have traffic.''

''Oh, yes, we do. It's awful.''

''Well, that's not the point.'' Nick paced to the window and peered out at the quiet street. ''Did she accomplish *anything* today?''

''At therapy? Not much.'' She paused. ''Nickie?''

''Yes?''

''Will you go with me next time?''

He tried to smile. ''Sure.''

After he'd given Katie a sound talking-to—and taken away TV privileges for three days—he hurried to the den and sat at Chet's rolltop desk, staring at the phone.

He'd been trying to avoid Chelsea all week. That visit he'd paid her raised too many questions. Such as, did he love Grace Lockwood? And had he really kissed Chelsea as passionately as he remembered?

Nick groaned.

Neither he nor Grace had ever pretended to be starry-eyed lovers, and until recently he'd liked that arrangement just fine. When stars got in your eyes, reason flew out the window. You made mistakes and got hurt. Laura was proof-positive of that.

But now Nick wondered if he'd be satisfied married to someone he didn't love passionately. Grace elicited no deep, vital emotion from him—which would be perfectly all right, except that lately someone else did.

Nick felt increasingly confused. Grace was such a good, sure person, a safe harbor. How could he give her up for the thrill of a second adolescence?

On the other hand, was it fair to bury his life in a relationship of, at best, courteous compatibility? And what would he do with all these rising feelings he'd thought he'd lost forever?

He gripped the receiver. What he'd do, he decided, was not think about it right now. His attraction to Chelsea was bound to fizzle, anyway. Nothing like that ever lasted long. In the meantime, he'd be very careful, back off and use restraint. That's what he'd do.

"Hi, Chelsea? Nick here. Remember that idea you had about Katie going for a balloon ride? Well, I think I'm just about ready to let her. But we have to make her work for it. Can you tell me more about those tickets you make kids earn?"

EVEN BEFORE NICK REACHED the meadow, he realized this was going to be no ordinary balloon flight. The field was alive with people, vans and at least six or seven balloons in various stages of readiness.

"Hi, guys." Chelsea waved as Nick, Katie and Grace got out of the Volvo.

"What's going on?" Nick stood with his hands on his hips, smiling at the dazzling colors and whimsical designs shimmering against the sky.

"I thought Katie'd get a kick out of it."

"Amazing." Nick knew he was grinning like a fool but couldn't stop. "Who are these people?"

"Friends. We get together whenever we can. Ballooning's more fun in a group. Larry's here, too, with his new balloon."

Chelsea looked pretty, Nick thought. Achingly pretty. Her outfit consisted of nothing more elaborate than sneakers, a plain yellow T-shirt and drawstring crinkle-cotton pants in the same soft shade. And his earrings, he noticed. Still, Nick had trouble keeping his face composed as he gazed at her.

Katie ran over and hugged Chelsea's waist. "I can't believe it. I can't believe it's finally happening." Then she danced off in search of Larry's boys.

"How did she do this week?" Chelsea asked over the sound of the fan.

"I thought she'd wear out the equipment. She kept hollering to the nurses, 'Am I doing good, huh? Do I get a ticket? Make sure you tell my dad I'm doing good.' She had everyone rooting for her."

Chelsea's laugh, her bright eyes and peach-fresh scent all combined to deal him a dizzying punch.

"Can I help out?" he asked.

"You bet."

Nick glanced guiltily at Grace, standing by the car.

"Go. Go." Grace fluttered one hand. "I'm fine."

But was she? She looked so out of place in her white ruffled blouse and gray pleated skirt. Her white pumps and nylons were no match for the rough field, either.

She could've stayed home, Nick thought. All week she'd made it clear she didn't approve of this flight. She'd called it dangerous and, since Nick was paying Katie's way, a terrible waste of money. Her face had remained pinched, her silences drawn out. She shouldn't have insisted on coming along. Nick had to wonder if she just wanted to make him feel guilty.

Katie was beside herself with excitement by the time Chelsea's balloon was ready. She'd been climbing incessantly in and out of the basket and asking one question after another. "I can't believe it!" she kept crying.

Nick's pleasure would've been complete if it weren't for Grace's calling to Katie just as incessantly to sit down and rest, or to zip up her jacket and put on her hat. She'd bought Katie a hat he'd never seen any other seven-year-old wearing. When he'd questioned Grace about it, she'd said it was to protect Katie from earache. Then just before Katie climbed into the basket to take off, Grace rushed over with an extra sweater.

"Will you leave the kid alone!" Nick finally hollered.

Grace reared back, stunned, and then looked as if she
might cry. Nick felt miserable. He'd never raised his voice
to her before. Why now? She was only trying to be helpful.

"Sorry, Grace, but it's a warm evening," he explained in
a conciliatory tone, "and Katie's already wearing a jacket."

"Fine." She spit the word out like a bitter seed. "Fine,"
she repeated and walked off with stiff little steps.

"Grace."

She turned.

"Want to give it a try?" Nick jerked his thumb toward the
waiting basket.

"No, thank you." Such cold pride in that voice.

He pulled in a long breath and turned toward Chelsea,
who was trying to act as if she hadn't heard. "Mind if I go
up with you and Katie? I suddenly feel the need for a balloon ride."

Frowning thoughtfully, Chelsea asked, "Are you sure?"

"Yes." Nick was dead sure.

The ride was different from Nick's first flight, but every
bit as wonderful. He found himself laughing exuberantly
when the signal was given and all seven balloons began to
ascend. His deepest joy, however, came from watching Katie. He'd never seen her this animated, her eyes so bright.

Larry had his sons with him, and Chelsea let Katie talk to
them briefly over the radio. When the two balloons drifted
only yards apart, Chelsea had the children in a fit of giggles
as she played "elevators" with her brother.

"Sixth floor. Lingerie," she called as they rose and Larry's balloon drifted downward. Then, reversing direction,
"Second floor. Pots, pans, kitchen utensils." Soon the
children were imitating her.

Nick stood by in something akin to awe. Chelsea had
quite a way with kids. As they passed over Pine Ridge she
pointed out things he wasn't aware of himself. A rock for-
mation that resembled a man's profile. A cave on the sheer

side of a hill. She called it Fairy's Flute because of the sound the wind made passing through it.

"Some people say they've heard the sound even when there isn't any wind," she said, her cheek pressed close to Katie's. "People say they've seen bright little lights, too, dancing inside the cave."

Katie's eyes grew larger with each word.

She sailed them over a lake, her balloon and all the others mirrored on the bright rippled surface below. She brought the basket down until they actually rested on the lake and water seeped through the wicker. Katie shrieked in delight, while Nick worried that perhaps something had gone wrong.

When she fired up the burner, however, he knew this was all part of her gift to Katie. As the basket rose, long chains of water streamed away, catching the low slanting sun like fiery strings of diamonds.

She took them over an orchard, which from the air seemed like a cloud of blossoms. Their fragrance perfumed the warm evening. Katie smiled, enraptured, as Chelsea brought them down right into the narrow corridor between two rows of trees. Blossoms surrounded them on either side, so close that Chelsea was able to snap off a small branch. It formed a full bouquet.

"Here you go, Katie. A souvenir."

She kept them aloft for two glorious hours. Still, time passed too quickly for Nick. Before he knew it, he was back on the ground, Judy and Rob were dismantling equipment, and he was feeling an ache return to his heart. Grace, more tenacious than he'd ever figured her to be, had followed the balloon and now was persistently calling Katie to the car.

But Katie was having none of it. She was too busy helping with the packing up.

"Katie, let's go. Nickie? We have to get home."

Nick was still savoring his champagne and thinking of having another glass. He looked from Katie to Grace with mounting frustration. "Grace, slow down. Come have a drink."

"No, thanks. I have a casserole waiting."

Nick pressed a hand to his cheek where a muscle was beginning to jump. "She's having fun, Grace. Let her be."

Rob and Judy were just rolling the basket onto the trailer. "Want to come out for pizza with us, instead?" Judy inquired.

A moment later, Katie was circling her father. "Can we, Dad? They're all going. Matt told me."

Nick's attention shifted from his daughter to Grace. She'd been driving for two hours and looked like she wanted to be home.

"Aw, come on," Judy prodded. "Who feels like cooking on a Saturday night?"

"It's a nice family restaurant," Larry called, crossing the field where he, too, had landed. "We usually go there after ballooning on Saturdays. The kids look forward to it."

Nick was amazed at how much like a kid he felt himself. He wanted . . . no, he *had* to go. He'd miss something important if he didn't. He gazed instinctively at Chelsea and knew exactly what that was.

"Grace? How about it?" Nick held his breath.

"If you want to go, then go, but I'm leaving." Grace got into his car and waited, her face pinched and red.

Nick knew he was facing a choice, knew something was hanging in the balance. He supposed the right thing to do was put down this champagne and leave.

But he didn't. Grace was playing on his guilt—and hurting Katie in the process.

"Okay, Grace," he called as congenially as he could. "I'll catch a ride home with somebody here."

She gave him, and then Chelsea, a malicious look before driving off.

THE RESTAURANT WAS a small, unassuming building sitting in the middle of its gravel parking lot on a winding rural road. But it was known for its good food, and Chelsea felt lucky to get a table without a wait. There were ten in her party tonight—Larry's family, Judy and Rob...and then there were Nick and Katie. Chelsea's heart raced at the thought of their actually being part of her family's Saturday night.

She'd had mixed feelings about piloting Katie's flight, not because of Katie, certainly; it was Nick she'd been reluctant to face again. She didn't understand what was happening between them.

Here was this man who'd once called her business a parasite, this man who was pulling away all the underpinnings of her life—her field, her sign, her home and barn—and setting her on the road to financial ruin. Here was this man who was practically engaged to Grace Lockwood, and yet she still had a crush on him.

No. Not a crush. She'd had crushes before, so she knew the difference. This condition wasn't going away. Rather, it was growing, becoming obsessive, and while it was all very thrilling, it was also very wrong.

More than a week had passed since Nick's strange visit, and during that time he hadn't said another word to her about the intimacy they'd shared, which obviously meant he wanted to let the whole incident slide. Well, fine. She agreed. It had been a mistake. She didn't know how it had happened in the first place.

Had she provoked the situation? Had she been forward? She couldn't judge anymore. Whenever she was with Nick, common sense flew out the window, and that was precisely what she had to guard against tonight.

Chelsea opened a menu. No, she hadn't been forward. She'd seen desire in his eyes even as he'd stepped into her house. *He* was the one who had initiated the visit, *he* who'd gone to answer a false alarm with a gift of earrings in his pocket. She wasn't imagining things. For weeks Nick Tanner had been sending her all the right signals. Only problem was, he kept going home to the wrong girl.

"I think I'll have a combination tonight, mushroom and pepperoni," Mimi said.

"Sounds good. Mind if I split it with you?" Rob asked from his end of the table. Chelsea concentrated on the menu.

But her mind was too full of Nick Tanner. The balloon ride had been fairly uncomplicated, with Katie along as a chaperon. Nick was a quiet person, given to long silences, and he hadn't said much. Still, she'd felt close, connected to him. Sharing the same experience had been enough to bind them in their own communication. Like wheels turning in unison, she thought. Like shadow dancers.

Still, the feeling was all wrong, and she'd better concentrate on sitting tight tonight and holding in whatever was in her heart. Otherwise, she'd make a fool of herself in front of her family.

Judy leaned toward her. "Care to split a sausage and onion?"

Chelsea considered, then shook off the proposal. "Tonight I'm in the mood for the works." Having made a decision, she closed the menu and sat back. Her eyes linked with Nick's. He smiled, and an absurd contentment washed through her even while she was trying to deny it.

"I hope you're real hungry, sis," Larry said.

Chelsea searched the faces around the table. "Aw, come on. I can't be the only one who likes the works."

"Yeah, you are," a few voices answered.

"I'll make a deal with you," Nick offered with a flirtatious wink. "Omit the anchovies and I'll split it with you."

The contentment she felt deepened to a mysterious excitement. "It's a deal, mister." She almost winked back but caught herself just in time. Nick didn't mean anything by that wink or that bone-melting smile. *Keep your head,* she cautioned herself. *Remember your dignity.*

Meanwhile, the logistics of deciding who wanted which pizza toppings was becoming ludicrous. "Okay, Matt, Peter and Katie want cheese and hamburg..." Larry had pulled out a pen and was jotting the order on a paper napkin "—and Judy's the only one who wants—"

"Wait a sec," Mimi cut in. "Change mine to..."

The shifting had been going on for so long, everybody was now laughing. An old rhythm-and-blues number pulsing from a jukebox across the dance floor, added to their festive mood.

Larry pushed his glasses up his nose and poised the napkin. "Grab hold of a waitress before someone here has a change of heart." A waitress heard him and hurried over, grinning.

"To make things easier, we really should sit beside the people we're sharing our pizzas with," Judy said when the waitress had gone. "Otherwise, hands are gonna be reaching all over the place."

A wave of groans and laughter overtook them again as they got up and rearranged themselves.

Chelsea's heart began to pound as soon as Nick got up to move. *Be calm,* she told herself. The man was only going to share her pizza.

But the damnable part about being attracted to someone, she realized, was that her mind could vow to do one thing and her heart did just what it pleased. At that moment, she suspected even her scalp must be pink.

"Nick, how are things coming along at Pine Ridge?" Larry inquired, fastening a bib around his daughter's neck.

Nick leaned slightly forward to answer, and his arm came in contact with Chelsea's. Neither of them seemed to breathe. He said something, and Larry said something back, but it was all a blur. Chelsea's whole existence centered on that warm, secret touch.

Suddenly she felt someone's attention. She glanced up to find her sister-in-law, Mimi, looking from her to Nick with an astonished little smile. Chelsea snapped to immediately. She was doing it. Somehow she was letting her feelings for Nick show. She folded her hands in her lap and assumed as sedate an expression as possible.

She picked up the conversation at " ... so, you figure construction'll start sometime next month?"

"Next month!" Chelsea swung around to catch Nick's nod. "Do I have to be out of the house that soon?"

Nick's gaze seemed to caress her. "Not yet."

She felt mesmerized, caught within a communication she didn't understand. She wanted to be angry with him; she wanted to fight, but couldn't.

"I hope you realize how difficult you've made Chelsea's life." Mimi's coy glance gave Chelsea the impression she was testing them.

"How so?" he asked.

"Well, it's obvious she'll never find a place as reasonable or as well situated as the house she's in now. Her business is bound to suffer."

Chelsea's cheeks grew hot. This was not a subject she cared to get into.

"Not if she broadens her horizons," Nick replied.

"How's she supposed to do that?" Mimi chewed on a smile as he moved his arm along the back of Chelsea's chair.

"Nick thinks I should become bolder in my business approach," Chelsea offered sardonically. "So, what do you figure? Full-color, tri-fold brochures placed in tourist centers across seven states? A couple of twelve-passenger gondolas and that new van I've been salivating over for two years?"

Nick's eyes glittered. "Go on and laugh, but sometimes a person has to go out on a limb in order to—"

"—fall flat on her face," Chelsea finished.

Their food arrived just then, and Nick dropped the subject until they'd all dug in. "Regarding Chelsea's business...I think she should consider other options."

"Like what?" Larry handed the baby a soft piece of cheese.

"Like contracting with a few bed-and-breakfasts in the area and offering a ballooning tour."

"A what?" Chelsea didn't care for the serious turn this conversation had taken.

"A tour. Passengers could be ballooned from one B-and-B to the next..."

"Sure." Larry nodded in agreement. "You could arrange sight-seeing trips when they land, side trips into shopping areas..."

Chelsea noticed Mimi watching her and Nick again. She had a distinct What's-going-on-with-you-two? look in her eyes.

Rob put down his beer. "What Chelsea really should do is get herself invited into Pine Ridge."

Chelsea swallowed her pizza with a loud gulp.

"What do you mean?" Nick's dark brows nearly met.

"Hasn't it occurred to you? Lots of ski areas have hot-air balloons as an added feature. Steamboat Springs in Colorado, for instance. They do it up real big."

"He's right." Larry chuckled. "But you'd better do it fast, before the idea becomes old hat. I was just reading about some place in the Adirondacks that's going to be offering balloon flights soon."

Chelsea knew the place. She'd seen their ad for pilots in a trade magazine just days ago.

But Nick didn't have room for Balloon the Berkshires at Pine Ridge, and more importantly, he didn't have the inclination. Chelsea's eyes pleaded with her family to quit the joke.

The waitress appeared again. "Can I get you folks anything else?"

"Yes, the children want ice cream." Nick seemed relieved to be interrupted.

Conversation veered onto safer subjects after that, and soon it was just another Saturday night with her family, children making perhaps too much noise, Rob and Judy trading off sick jokes, everyone warm and comfortable with each other—including Nick, she noticed with an oddly piercing pleasure. He really looked relaxed, loosened like she'd never seen him before. It wasn't just the jeans and sweatshirt he was wearing. There was a lightheartedness—a glow—that had nothing to do with his clothes.

Music was still pulsing from the old jukebox, one classic rock-and-roll number after another. When "Johnny Be Good" came on, Nick pushed back his chair. "Hell! How can anybody sit when that song's playing? I've got to dance. Someone here humor me, please." He stood up and held a hand toward Chelsea, one eyebrow cocked in the most knee-weakening invitation she'd ever encountered.

She was out of her seat in a flash.

It was uncanny how well they danced together, she thought as the loud, driving music enveloped them. She anticipated every move he made. When the record finished, he guided her over to the jukebox, his arm never leaving her waist, and slipped in another coin. Laughing, they started to dance again.

By the time they returned to the table, her cheeks were red-hot and she was almost out of breath. Everyone cheered them with a noisy round of applause.

"What a bunch of rowdies," Chelsea chided. Even the baby was clapping. Chelsea kissed her plump cheek and sat down, sighing happily. "You got the check? Oh, great. This should be rich. Get out the calculator, Lar."

Her laughter died, however, when she realized Mimi was no longer the only one giving her and Nick a curious look. She folded her hands in her lap and tried to calm down. Maybe she shouldn't have danced with Nick; at least she shouldn't have been so eager. She searched her heart for feelings of remorse, but there were none to be found. Dancing with him had been too much fun. It had felt too right.

She thought of the guys she sometimes dated. They were all handsome, popular, yet she'd never been attracted to them the way she was to Nick. She'd known a few since childhood, but they still weren't as close. They were convenient, that's what they were; always available when she needed a date.

Well, that wasn't enough anymore. In spite of everything she'd ever said about not wanting a relationship because of her business, she wasn't satisfied just biding her time. She wanted to get on with the real thing. She wanted to be like her brother and sister, to share her life with someone she loved and have a home of her own, a real home. And Lord, how she longed for kids. She'd never dreamed she'd ever want them this much. But most of all she wanted the breathless excitement she'd felt in Nick's arms. She wanted . . .

Chelsea started. What had she just called it? *The real thing?* She turned her eyes on Nick just as he looked at her. Yes, it did feel real, didn't it? Real and forever. It felt like they should be leaving together, going home somewhere. She could see them spending another evening like this in five years, and another in twenty-five. Real. Forever. Good heavens, she was in love with Nick Tanner! In that brief exchange of glances, the realization struck her with all the certainty of a freight train. She *loved* him.

She had the feeling he might be able to love her, too, if only he'd give himself the chance, but that didn't seem likely. He'd obviously formed an idea of the perfect wife, and Grace Lockwood, for some reason, fit the bill.

"Well, if you folks don't mind, we're going to be heading home," Rob said.

"Yeah, us, too," Mimi added. "Nick, will Chelsea be dropping you and Katie off?"

A slight tension buzzed the air. Chelsea knew everyone was opening the way for her and Nick to be together. All they had to do was walk into the invitation.

"Uh . . . I don't think so. Larry, would you give us a lift? We're more on your way."

Chelsea didn't look at anyone. Nick, of course, was making the right decision. They'd shared a pleasant evening, but now it was time to get back to reality. A few covert glances, a dance or two...but he had to return to Grace.

Chelsea reeled with confusion. What kind of game was he playing? How could they share so much, and Grace still hold claim to his heart?

Apparently, Grace had something that Nick needed, and Chelsea wished she knew what it was.

"Good night, Chelse," he called as he and Katie followed Larry across the parking lot.

She waved, but he never turned around.

CHAPTER ELEVEN

ALMOST A WEEK PASSED before Chelsea talked to Nick again.

"Hi, Chelsea? Nick."

In her joy, she almost dropped the phone. "Hi."

"Hi. Listen, I have a favor to ask. Your van *is* running okay these days, isn't it?"

"Yes."

"May I borrow it?"

She tried to steady her breathing. "Depends on when."

"Tomorrow afternoon."

"Fine by me."

"Great. I have a few things back in Boston I'd like to get out of storage. Summer clothes, my stereo, stuff like that. Nothing that'll do in your shocks or springs."

"I'm not concerned." She wondered why he was borrowing her old clunker. He could afford a fleet of U-Hauls.

"Chelsea?"

She didn't answer right away. She loved hearing him say her name and didn't want to spoil the afterglow. "Yes."

"I have another favor to ask. Can I borrow you, too?"

"What did you say?"

"I'm having the gas turned on at my apartment tomorrow, and since I won't be there, I was wondering if..."

"If I could wait around hours and hours for the gas man to show up."

"Yes."

"What's in it for me?" She rested her forehead against the window and smiled at the lilacs bobbing in the late May breeze.

"How about . . . Chinese?"

"Do I get fortune cookies, too?"

"I guess."

"And do you guarantee I'll get the fortune I want?"

"Absolutely!"

"Then you've got yourself a deal."

There, they were at it again, bantering like a couple of junior-high sweethearts. But why? Nick was a pretty savvy guy. He must sense what was happening. Did he just enjoy leading her on? she wondered. No, being a flirt wasn't in his nature. Then, did he really feel something for her but not know what to do about it? Was he torn, straddling a fence?

"What time do you need the van?"

"Twelve, one o'clock?"

"Okay. I'll have it ready."

"Uh, Chelse?"

"What?" She was afraid she'd say something stupid if they didn't cut this short.

"It might be easier if you come by the apartment and I take the van from there."

"Oh, right."

"I can leave you my car."

"Makes sense."

"So, tomorrow."

"Yes, around noon."

"Chelse?"

"Yes?" Her voice whispered with anticipation. How she wanted to stay on the line.

"How've you been?"

She closed her eyes, silently answering, *Terrible. I'm in love with you.* What she let herself say was "Fine."

"Well, good. Okay, then I'll see you tomorrow."

She nodded and hung up the phone.

WHERE WAS SHE? Nick wondered for the hundredth time that hour. He turned from the window and paced. Not that Chelsea was late; he was simply overeager.

Nick forced himself to sit in one of the club chairs that came with the apartment. He told himself the only business he had with Chelsea today was her van, but his fingers kept tapping the upholstered arm, and his heart knew better.

Ever since they'd taken Katie ballooning, he'd been wondering when he could see her again. She'd driven him crazy that evening. He hadn't expected his reaction to be so strong, but he should have. Everytime he was with her it got worse, and that evening in the restaurant, he'd had all he could do to keep track of conversation and hide the thoughts and urges that were straining to be released.

Sometime during that evening, he'd decided he'd have to talk to Grace. He couldn't go on pretending he was interested in marrying her. At the moment he wasn't interested in marrying anyone. He and Katie would do just fine on their own.

Right now what he needed was the freedom to explore the excitement Chelsea was raising in his blood. He'd have to be careful, of course. Theirs was only a physical attraction, and he refused to let it grow into anything more. Loving someone, being totally involved in and responsible for another person's life—that was still a scenario he wanted to avoid.

This fire in his blood, though—he wouldn't fight it anymore. It had been so long since he'd felt it, so long since he'd felt anything except the need to work and provide and be responsible. He'd forgotten that he *could* feel, or that he needed to in order to be whole.

Nick knew that whatever he and Chelsea shared could go nowhere, but he didn't think she'd mind. She'd told him herself she wasn't interested in serious relationships. Her top priority was her business. They'd talk about it this evening when he got back. That was the best way, being open, getting the ground rules straight before they embarked on anything.

He only wished he'd gotten to talk to Grace first. He'd fully intended to, the night he and Katie returned from the restaurant. He'd put Katie to bed and gone down to look for Grace, but apparently she'd already turned in. And then the next evening, when he'd been waiting for her to join him in the den, he'd happened upon her old yearbook. Chelsea's yearbook, too. By the time Grace had walked in, he'd been so lost in his obsession to unearth Chelsea's past, every last photo, every activity, boyfriend, prom dress, favorite song...

He'd looked up, startled, caught, but Grace had startled him even more by breaking into a smile. "Checking to see what I looked like ten years ago?" He hadn't had the heart to say no.

A vehicle came to a stop below his front window. Nick shot from his chair and peered down to the curb. Chelsea was just getting out of her van, looking more beautiful than he remembered. The earth began to spin as crazily as his heart was pounding. He would definitely have to talk to Grace soon.

"Hi, come on in."

Chelsea stepped over the threshold, her big gray eyes scanning the living room. "Hmm. Very nice."

"Yeah?"

"Yeah. Here, I brought you some flowers. A housewarming gift." Her dark lashes fluttered as she cast her eyes down. With self-consciousness? Nick wondered.

"Thank you. I've never received flowers from a lady before. Let me put them in water."

"They're for the house. The apartment, I mean." Yes, she was definitely nervous. "When are you moving in?"

"I might stay here tonight."

"Grace is going to miss you."

Nick shrugged evasively as he set the flowers on the coffee table. Chelsea was wearing a pink shirt today the exact shade as her cheeks. It was oversized but still didn't hide the most enticingly fitted jeans he'd ever beheld. He'd better be leaving, if he wanted to leave at all.

"Well, I'm off." He flipped her keys in his hand. "The trip should take at lease five hours, maybe six."

"Don't speed."

"I won't. My car's out front, keys on the kitchen table. If the gas man finishes up early and you want to go home..." Nick didn't finish the sentence. He couldn't bear the idea of her not being here when he got back.

CHELSEA'S EYES ROAMED Nick's apartment. He'd chosen a lovely place, even though it was only transitional—large, sunny, beautifully furnished. She strolled from room to room. His rooms, where he'd eat and sleep and play with Katie. She paused in the kitchen doorway, savoring an image of him sitting at the table. Dreamily, she walked in and, thinking of all the meals that would be prepared here, brushed her fingers over the counter.

Immediately she pulled her hand back. The counter wasn't the cleanest thing in the world, she noticed in surprise. Neither was the stove. She surveyed the rest of the appliances, then returned to the living room. Actually, the whole place was in need of a cleaning, and it grieved her to think of Nick and Katie—especially Katie—moving into a place that wasn't ready.

Tonight? Did he really mean to stay here tonight? There wasn't a crumb of food in the kitchen. Beds weren't made, and the shower stall smelled sour.

She opened the cabinet under the bathroom sink. But of course. The one thing the landlord had provided was lots of cleaning products. Smiling in disbelief at what she was about to do, Chelsea reached for a scrub brush.

NICK HAD GOTTEN RID of most of his furniture when he sold his house. Still, the little he'd kept filled the van, and packing it took longer than he expected. He'd have to skip that visit to the bank he'd vaguely planned—which was just as well; he wasn't dressed for hobnobbing with his old friends. Besides, catching up on the latest scuttlebutt didn't seem all that important anymore, and between Boston and the Berkshires lay a mighty long piece of road.

Nick kept to the speed limit because he was driving Chelsea's van, but never for a minute did he stop wanting to floor the gas pedal. By the time he reached the foothills, he wished the damn thing could fly. Boston wasn't home anymore. It was just a big, busy city where once he'd happened to live. The Berkshires was where he belonged now, this timeless area of mountains and lakes, of covered bridges and Norman Rockwell villages, of new friends and work that was finally satisfying. And Chelsea.

He smiled as he thought of the evening ahead. His stereo equipment was jiggling somewhere at the back of the van, along with his collection of music. He would set that up first thing, and as they ate he'd gradually expose her to the fact that he had a thing about Brazilian music. But it would be all right if she didn't like sambas. He had rock. He had classical. Anything she wanted.

He had gone a little overboard at the Chinese restaurant, he decided, grinning at the three brown bags on the seat beside him. But he wasn't sure what she liked, so he'd bought a little of everything.

That was okay. They had time to eat slowly. All the time in the world. Katie had stayed with Grace this afternoon, but Larry was picking her up for dinner and a "sleepover" at his house.

He'd suggest they eat in the living room, on the floor. They'd lower the lights, kick off their shoes and settle down to a casual—no, a Bohemian—feast.

He could see it now, actually felt tension uncoiling just at the thought. It would be laid-back and spontaneous. A Chelsea kind of evening.

And after that, when they'd eaten their fill and talked enough about nothing, he'd broach the subject of beginning an affair. He didn't think she'd object. Of course, he'd have to be honest and discuss all the ground rules. He didn't want either of them to risk getting serious.

And then . . . ?

Nick sucked in his breath as a bolt of fire flashed straight through him. Lord, how he wished this old van could fly.

CHELSEA STARED at her reflection in the bathroom mirror and groaned. "You're a wreck, Lawton." Her shirt was filthy, her face sagged with tiredness, and her hands looked like hamburger.

But at least the apartment was ready for Nick and Katie to move in. Her energy and efficiency had thoroughly amazed her. She'd even run out to the market for food, staples to get them through tomorrow, and tonight's dinner, which was in the oven now.

She smiled, imagining Nick's surprise when he walked in the door. He'd check out the polished rooms, sniff the aromatic chicken, gaze at the beautifully set table, and his pleasure would be all the thanks she'd need.

She'd sit him down and serve him dinner, maybe unpack his clothes while he ate. Moving was such a chore; he was sure to appreciate the help.

And after he'd eaten and she was clearing the dishes, maybe they'd have a chance to talk. She sorely wanted to dispel the misconceptions he had about her. She was a responsible woman, a serious person, not a flighty kid. She wanted him to know they shared the same ideals—of home and work and family.

And after the talk . . . ?

Chelsea didn't know what she hoped for then. Approval? A new respect? His acceptance of her as the sort of woman he could love? Her smile softened.

But first, she really had to do something about these clothes. She checked her watch. Still time to zip home and change.

HE KNOCKED FIRST. "Chelse?"

"Coming."

The door opened and Nick felt an almost uncontrollable urge to scoop Chelsea into his arms. But in the very same moment, an assortment of fragrances assailed his senses. Strong scents like bleach and furniture polish, freshly baked cake and barbecue sauce.

"You made good time." Chelsea smiled expectantly.

"Wasn't much traffic." He dropped the bags of food on the coffee table and took a quick sweeping look at the room, then at her. "You changed your clothes."

She looked very nice. Too nice. She was wearing a rather dressy turquoise sheath, pearls, prim white pumps, and she'd put on makeup. Lipstick, eyeshadow, the whole works.

"Are you going somewhere?" he asked.

"No." She chewed on her lip, and he sensed disappointment had slipped into his expression.

"Well, good. You look nice." Untouchable, unkissable—but nice. "What have you been doing while I was gone?"

"Oh, just a little straightening up. I got restless."

"Holy..." Nick couldn't believe the extent of her "straightening up." One look at her hands told him the rest of the story. She looked tired, too. The dream that had kept him going all that day began to unravel.

"Did the gas man come?"

"Uh-huh."

Of course he had. Nick could smell food cooking. He gave the bags on the coffee table a disappointed glance.

She followed his gaze. "What's that?"

"Uh...Chinese."

"Oh." She looked rather disappointed herself. "I noticed you didn't have any food, so I went out and got a few things. I didn't think you and Katie would appreciate waking up tomorrow to an empty cupboard. I hope you don't mind, but I got a little something for dinner, too."

Nick felt a knot of frustration tightening inside. This wasn't the sort of evening he'd envisioned. "I told you yesterday I'd get Chinese."

She wrung her fingers. "I forgot. Sorry. But that's okay. Now you and Katie'll have lots of leftovers the rest of the week."

Nick walked into the kitchen, almost afraid of what he might find. Sure enough, the table in the dining alcove was set—flowers, candles, napkin fanning perfectly from a wineglass. The floor had been washed, too, and a chocolate cake was cooling on the counter.

"Chelsea, for heaven's sake. What have you been doing?"

She followed him into the kitchen, a little unsteadily, he thought. She bit her lip again and grimaced. "You don't like barbecued chicken?"

Nick rubbed a hand over his face. "No. Yes. I mean it's fine. But you shouldn't have gone to all this trouble."

"My pleasure," she said softly, but he noticed her exuberance was gone.

"Is there enough time for me to move some things up from the van before we eat?"

She glanced at the stove and shrugged uncertainly.

"I just thought it'd be nice to hook up my stereo..."

"Stereo? Wouldn't you rather leave that till last? It's not exactly the most essential thing..."

Okay, so there'd be no spontaneous dinner on the floor, and there'd be no Brazilian sambas. Nick pulled in a deep breath and exhaled it slowly.

"I hope you have some sheets down in the van. There aren't any on the beds, you know."

"Yes, I think I do."

"Good. While you're eating, I'll fix up your beds."

"Aren't you going to join me?"

"Maybe for dessert."

Okay. So there'd be no Chelsea, either. He yanked out a chair and said goodbye to the last of his fantasy.

"Would you like the Chinese food or what I cooked?"

"Yes, that." He pointed distractedly toward the oven.

"The chicken turned out okay, but I'm afraid I burned the rolls." She carried her head so stiffly. What on earth was the matter with her?

From the refrigerator, she pulled a bottle of chilled white wine. Nick had had enough. "What are you doing, Chelsea?"

"What do you mean?" She sounded as if her throat was closing.

"I mean this." He indicated the entire gleaming room with a sweeping gesture of one arm. "And this." He plucked at her turquoise skirt. "Hell, I go away for six hours and you turn into June Cleaver!"

Chelsea lowered the wine bottle slowly, her jaw wobbling.

"I'm sorry." Nick raked his hair back and sighed. "But you've obviously been knocking yourself out today, and I can't figure out why. This place has a cleaning service, you know. They just haven't had a chance to come in yet."

"Where are your sheets?" Chelsea looked up at the ceiling rather than meet his gaze.

"Behind the driver's seat. White bag."

She nodded and clopped off, head still held high.

Nick hardly tasted anything he ate. He kept listening to Chelsea bumping around his bedroom. Finally he threw down his napkin and strode out of the kitchen.

She was just tucking the spread over the pillows of his bed. Though she wasn't making a sound, tears were sliding down her cheeks.

CHELSEA'S GAZE shot up. Nick was standing in the doorway, watching her. Great. As if she hadn't made enough of a fool of herself! She'd thought she was doing him a favor, cleaning the apartment, cooking his dinner. She'd thought he'd be so pleased.

It wasn't until he'd returned, however, and she'd seen herself through his eyes, that she'd realized what a jerk she was. Nick's face had said it all. She was a clown, fussing around his apartment like some sitcom caricature of a housewife.

And why? As Chelsea gazed at Nick standing in the doorway, she knew the answer clearly. She wanted to be the woman of Nick's house. She wanted to share his life, but since she didn't fit his image of Mrs. Perfect, she'd tried to imitate the woman who did.

Nick crossed the room in three long strides and gripped her by the arms. "What's wrong?" He leaned close, peering into her eyes.

"I should go...." She tried to pull away, but he only held her tighter.

"Nick, please."

"What's wrong?" His fingers dug deeper.

Chelsea looked up. Nick was everything she ever wanted in life—and would never have. "Everything," she finally admitted, her voice catching on a sob. "Just about everything. I'm sorry, Nick. I didn't mean to insinuate myself into your home, into your kitchen and all." She wished her mouth would stop trembling. "I had no right. It was presumptuous. We really don't know each other well enough for me to have done what I did."

Nick tilted his dark head, a strange little smile breaking through his concern. "Oh, Chelsea. You think I was upset because you'd...you'd insinuated yourself?"

"You're not?"

He dropped his forehead to hers. "No. I was looking forward to a different sort of evening, and I was frustrated. That's all. I didn't want you cleaning. I didn't want you cooking. I just...wanted your company tonight."

This admission touched off a response in Chelsea she didn't anticipate. She wasn't sure if she was sad or happy; she only knew she couldn't keep from breaking down.

Nick folded her close, rocking her gently as she cried.

"I f-feel s-so stupid," she sobbed into his chest.

He smoothed back her hair, stroked the length of her back. "Shh. I don't want to hear it."

"I'm getting your shirt all wet," she choked out.

"I almost care."

For some reason, this made her laugh. Nick lowered his head and brushed his cheek against hers. He pressed his lips to her hair. Chelsea snuggled closer. Nick was warm and safe—exactly where she wanted to be.

"Oh, Chelsea," he whispered shakily, and the next moment his lips were touching hers.

Nick feared she would push him away. He hadn't meant to kiss her then, but he couldn't help it. Holding her in his arms, feeling her press against him, he'd just lost all control.

Chelsea didn't resist. Rather, she wrapped her arms around his neck and pressed closer. Nick moaned, feeling the fire he'd been banking since the day they'd first met blaze into an inferno. He wanted to kiss her everywhere, touch her everywhere. To his astonishment, she seemed to feel the same.

He finally managed to pull away from the kiss, and she dropped her head to his chest. He could feel her heart hammering.

"I just couldn't hold back anymore," he whispered against the soft crown of her hair. "I'm sorry. You drive me crazy."

She smiled, gazing into his eyes with a look that turned his knees to mush. Nick wondered how he'd ever thought he could live without this.

He kissed her again, savoring the taste of her, the feel of her. He moved his hands along her back to her head, his fingers threading through the thick silk of her hair. The kiss deepened, and he heard her whimper. At that moment, the world swirled away, leaving them on an island that consisted solely of sensual contact.

The dress she wore was soft, silky. It slid like hot fluid beneath his exploring hands. The material was thin, and through it he could almost feel the pores of her skin. Yet it wasn't enough. If he wasn't careful, he was going to tear the damn thing right off her back.

He felt her press closer, her legs rubbing the coarse denim of his jeans. She overwhelmed him, swept him along on a tide as uncontrollable as an ocean surge.

This isn't the way it was supposed to happen, Nick thought. They were supposed to have music and egg rolls and conversation. But as she arched against him, her smooth, white neck inviting his kiss, he realized they didn't need any of those trappings. *Here* was the center of his dream, *here* the source of his need.

Chelsea was vaguely aware of being lifted off her feet. A moment later Nick lowered her onto his bed and settled alongside her. She snuggled closer, searching for his warmth.

He stroked back her hair, for a moment not kissing her but just gazing into her eyes. She stared at him, too, reeling in the intoxication caused by his attention. Her happiness was overwhelming.

"You're so beautiful..." His whisper was heartfelt, awestruck.

"You, too." The knuckle of her index finger trailed along his rough cheek to his jaw. She felt him shudder under the light touch, just before leaning over her to take her in another kiss.

He kept on kissing her, their hunger deepening until Chelsea was nearly mindless with it. This wasn't how she'd thought the evening would go. Their food was getting cold, they were messing the bed, her outfit was a shambles.

But when all was said and done, who cared? Nick was here with her, without the preliminaries, and that was all that mattered.

Vaguely she wondered where all this was leading, but she thought she already knew. For heaven's sake, they were already lying on the bed! There was no middle ground when it came to her and Nick. No dinner. No conversation. Just spontaneous combustion. She'd never known anything like it in her life. Would she stop him? she wondered, hearing the zipper whisper open down her back. Did she have the necessary self-control?

Nick eased her dress off her shoulders, over her arms, all the while kissing her with an intimacy that was causing major shock waves through her nervous system.

Would she stop him? she asked herself again. And the answer came back, Why *should* she? She loved seeing him happy, loved giving him pleasure. She suspected he hadn't allowed himself a whole lot of that during the past few years.

Her breathing was labored as she worked her hands under his T-shirt and over the hot, tensed muscles of his back. The next moment, he'd ripped off the shirt, and the crisp dark hair that matted his chest was prickling through the lace of her bra. Chelsea sank into the soft pillows, burning with sensations she'd never dreamed possible.

"I . . . I love your body," she whispered shyly, tracing the muscled curve of his neck.

She felt a reaction. "Chelsea, are you sure this is all right?"

"Oh, Nick," she cried, hugging him tight to her. "Of course it's all right. I love you. I *love* you." The words poured out like a song suppressed too long.

Nick lay very still, his cheek pressed to her ear. Chelsea waited—then tried to move. She wanted to seal her avowal of love with a kiss, a smile—something! But he'd stiffened into place, his breathing arrested.

His eyes were closed when he eased away from her onto his back, but she could still read his anguish. There and then, she knew she'd made one hell of a mistake.

SHE LOVED HIM? Nick dropped his arm over his face and prayed he was just dreaming. But of course he knew he wasn't. The heat of passion draining from his body was all too real, as real as the cold sweat of alarm that was replacing it.

The silence lengthened. Did he love her in return? Is that what he was supposed to say now? His blood began to pound. Damn! This never should've happened. If only he'd stuck to his plan, talked to her, set limits on what they could expect. But no, he'd had to throw caution to the wind.

"Nick?" Chelsea's voice sounded so small.

He turned to look at her, wishing there were some way to erase the last few minutes.

"Nick, I think someone's knocking at your door."

"Oh." He sat up, feeling cold and hollow. "Oh, yes." He tugged his shirt on and pushed a hand through his hair. "Are you all right?"

Chelsea sat up, not looking at him, and nodded. The turquoise dress lay in folds around her small waist. Her lips looked bee-stung, and her near-ebony hair fell in tousled shocks across her face. She looked more enticing than anyone he'd ever seen, but she'd also withdrawn into a hurt he knew he'd caused.

"Here, let me zip you up."

"No. I can manage." He didn't like the way she was avoiding his eyes. "Go answer your door."

He pulled in a breath. "All right. Be back soon."

Nick hurried off. He had a problem on his hands, one he didn't know how to solve. But he would. Chelsea was too important for him not to. He would, as soon as he got rid of whoever was pounding on his door.

He swung it open, and his heart plummeted, for there stood Grace Lockwood, hands on her hips and murder in her eyes.

CHAPTER TWELVE

CHELSEA ZIPPED UP her dress and sat on the bed again, tears of humiliation scalding her eyes. Had she really told Nick that she loved him? Had she been that out of control that she couldn't hold in the words? She'd never said them to anyone before. Why him? Why now?

She supposed everything would be different if only Nick had said he loved her, too. But he hadn't, and that was the crux of the matter. Nick didn't love her. She knew she had no right to expect him to. Still, it had hurt to feel him withdraw as if she'd done something repulsive. It hurt now.

She pressed her eyes with unsteady fingers and prayed for a way to erase the tension she'd created. She wanted them to return to where they'd been before she'd opened her mouth, but she feared it was too late.

Chelsea stiffened. She swore she heard Grace's voice. My Lord, it *was* Grace! At the door, talking to Nick. She'd forgotten all about Grace when she'd been in Nick's arms. Forgotten? Or had she just dismissed her as unimportant? Either way, Chelsea felt mortified.

Deep down, she'd never believed Nick loved Grace, and that, she supposed, was why she'd never been able to rouse any guilt. But Grace and Nick *were* involved, however thin the relationship, and she'd had no right to ignore the fact.

It didn't matter that Nick had ignored it himself. She wasn't responsible for what he did. But she was responsible for herself, and she'd acted reprehensibly.

She stood up on legs that quivered. Grace must know she was here. Her van was parked right out front. Would Grace believe an excuse? Could she think of a plausible one? She wanted to spare Grace's feelings if she could.

"Hi, Grace." Chelsea smiled, hoping she appeared to be coming from the kitchen.

Grace swung on her, her pale blue eyes burning with anger. Her mouth was so tight her lips had disappeared. One glance at the lipstick smudge on Nick's cheek, and Chelsea cringed.

"And I thought you were my friend," Grace seethed.

"You'd better go, Chelse," Nick warned. "Take my car. I'll call you later."

Was he trying to protect her from the bedlam that was about to erupt, or did he just want her out of the way so that he could comfort Grace without distraction?

"No, she might as well stay and hear this, too." Grace sounded vindictive.

Chelsea stepped closer. "What's the matter? Has something happened?"

"You bet something has. Katie's missing, that's what."

"What?" Nick demanded.

"She's taken off."

He gripped Grace's arm. "Where? When?"

"Around five. Two hours ago, I'd say."

Nick's color drained.

"We were at Pine Ridge. I had a little paperwork to do for Father. Nothing much. I was watching her, but somehow she managed to get away. She's really becoming incorrigible, Nickie, and I'm afraid certain people have only reinforced her notion that it's all right to break the rules." Her gaze slid to Chelsea again.

Nick grabbed his car keys and unceremoniously pushed Chelsea and Grace out the door. "Did you look for her?" he asked, racing down the stairs.

"Of course. And there are people looking now. The construction workers and grounds crew. I didn't want to alarm you. I thought she'd turn up by now."

"Get in," Nick growled as he threw himself behind the wheel of his car.

Sitting in the back seat, Chelsea felt like vomiting. Dear Lord, where *was* that child?

"Two hours! Dammit, Grace!" Nick jabbed the steering wheel with his fist. "Where was she when you last saw her?"

"The sitting area of Father's office. I was right in the next room."

"Did anybody come in? Anyone suspicious drive through?"

"No. No one."

Chelsea tried to think. There had to be a way of figuring this out. "What was she talking about this afternoon?"

"Oh, for pity's sake, Chelsea." Grace's voice rasped with impatience.

"Well, I just thought it might give us a clue. Maybe she wanted to do something, go somewhere."

Grace thought a while, none too seriously, in Chelsea's opinion. "She *was* chattering on about something. Flutes, I think it was. She wanted to hear flutes, she said." Grace tossed her head dismissively. Chelsea stopped breathing.

Nick's eyes were sharp and cold as he glanced over his shoulder. "Fairy's Flute. You think you can show us the way up there, Chelse?" His wrath, though tightly contained, was quelling.

"Yes."

"Fairy what? What are you talking about?"

"The cave out on the north ridge, Grace." Chelsea explained. "Overlooking the old quarry."

"Oh, yes. I know the one you mean. Oh, heavens! Why would Katie ever want to head out there? It's more than a mile away, through the woods. Not the safest area, either, what with the water in the quarry and the sheer rock face....

"Grace, will you shut up!" Chelsea blurted.

"Well, excuse me! But if it weren't for you, she probably never would've taken off in the first place. Ever since she skipped off from her father to go see your stupid balloon, she figures it's okay to do whatever she pleases. Your influence hasn't helped any, either."

"Enough, Grace," Nick said. "The important thing now is to find Katie." He didn't mention that Chelsea was also the one who'd told Katie about the cave, but Chelsea knew it lay heavily on his mind, just as it did on her own.

Chet stood on the deck of the main lodge, apparently acting as coordinator for the impromptu search. Nick listened as Chet explained how many people he'd rounded up and where they were looking.

"Call the police," Nick said in a voice that brooked no opposition. "Tell them to bring their bloodhounds. I don't want to waste any more time. This is too big an area, too much forest, and it'll be dark soon. Call the police." He was already running back to his car.

"Where ya going, son?"

"North, along the old quarry road. We think Katie may have taken a walk that way."

Chet looked disbelieving but didn't argue.

"Grace, will you stay here? The police will probably need some of Katie's clothing...."

"Yes, of course." Nick was about to get into his car when she threw her arms around his neck. "Be careful, Nickie."

Standing beside the car, Chelsea turned her face as heartache ripped through her.

"Okay, give me directions," Nick said as he slipped behind the wheel. Chelsea willed away her hurt and got in, too.

Chelsea wished she had her Jeep. The road they took was unpaved and rutted, and more than once she didn't think the Volvo would make it.

"Do you really think she headed this way?"

"I don't know." Nick pronounced each word with distinct anger. He was obviously in no mood to talk. Especially not to her.

The woods dipped to the right, a dense, trackless thicket that rolled on for miles. The sun had sunk behind the ridge and it was already dark beneath the trees. Chelsea shivered. She knew Nick was concerned about the deep, frigid water in the abandoned quarry. He was probably also worried about Katie's trying to climb the steep rocky slope up to the cave. What he hadn't considered, she suspected, were the woods, and she hoped he never did. In her estimation they presented a far greater danger.

"I'm sorry, Nick," she choked out.

His profile was unyieldingly grim. He just shook his head as if refusing to accept her apology.

"Now what do we do?" Nick peered through his dusty windshield as the road ended and they drove onto a scraped and scarred open area that had once been part of the quarry.

Chelsea answered by getting out and calling Katie's name as loud as she could. She was scared, more scared than she cared to admit. She wished she could do something more.

She envisioned herself gliding over the woods in her balloon and finding Katie, snatching her up from harm's way and becoming a heroine in Nick's eyes. But the reality was, not only would daylight be gone before she even got home to her equipment, but her vision was sheer, impossible folly born of desperation.

Her heart wrenched as she watched Nick peering down the embankment, littered with splintered granite, toward the dark pool. It was too much for one father to go through twice in a lifetime. She would never forgive herself for being the cause. And she was. Grace was right. He was right. She'd told Nick to give Katie more freedom, to let her get on with her life. Chelsea had encouraged adventure. If Nick had followed his own instincts, Katie would be safe at home now.

"Katie," she called almost desperately, suffering an image of the child lying hurt and unconscious somewhere. "Katie!"

Suddenly high on the breeze came a thin reply. "Hey!"

Nick and Chelsea both spun around, searching for the source of the sound.

"Hi! I'm up here!"

Chelsea's gaze scaled the steep grade up toward the cave, her alarm contending with relief. "Thank God!" she whispered, taking off up the jagged granite despite her silk dress and heels.

Nick passed her at a run. By the time she reached the top, he was sitting on the ground with Katie in his arms. Chelsea noticed his lashes were wet.

"Is she all right?" Chelsea had taken off her shoes, and her stockings were a mass of runs.

"I bumped my head." Katie's lower lip trembled. Indeed she had, Chelsea noticed. "And I don't know how to get down." Katie turned her tired, begrimed face into Nick's shirt and fought a bout with tears.

Chelsea cast a look down and wondered about the return trip herself.

"Chelsea?"

"Yes, honey."

"There aren't any fairies up here."

Chelsea thought her heart would break.

Nick's eyes narrowed to hard, angry slits. He'd moved beyond not loving her; now he despised her.

"Katie, it was very wrong to come up here. You know that, don't you?" she said.

A muscle jumped along Nick's jawline. "I'll handle Katie's discipline."

"I wasn't . . . I only . . ."

"You've done enough, now just leave her alone, okay?"

The ride back to the lodge passed in near silence. For a while, Katie chattered on about her hike, looking rather proud of her accomplishment. But soon she seemed to sense the tension between the two adults and fell silent.

As soon as they pulled up, people started rushing toward them. Chet, Grace, construction workers, the police who'd arrived while they were gone. Katie was thoroughly confused by the attention, and for a long while didn't understand she was the cause of it.

Chelsea drifted to the sidelines, ignored. She wasn't needed here anymore, and worse, she wasn't wanted. She had no place in the rejoicing.

"Hi, sis."

Chelsea's head jerked up. "Larry, what are you doing here?"

"I came by to get Katie. She was supposed to sleep over." From the looks of him, he'd been tramping through woods for the last two hours.

"Can you give me a lift home?" Chelsea asked. "I'm here without wheels."

"How come?"

"Long story. Will you do it, please?"

"Yeah, sure. Hey, are you okay?"

"No. Not okay at all."

Larry took her by the shoulders.

"Don't ask any questions. I just need to be alone."

He hesitated, then nodded. "Okay. Let's go."

CHELSEA WAVED GOODBYE to her brother from the front porch, thankful that he'd respected her desire not to be questioned. She was too upset to talk right now. Upset?

Actually she was coming apart at the seams. This day had been a disaster.

She cringed when she thought of all the cleaning and shopping and cooking she'd done. Not only were her hands blistered and her wallet lighter, but she'd acted such a fool, playing at "wifey" in some desperate attempt to impress Nick.

That, however, was the least of it, she thought, remembering the passionate encounter that had followed. She'd responded to Nick with an abandon that was humiliating. It was fairly obvious now that she had no control over herself when she was with him.

Then there was the issue of Grace, Grace walking in on their foolhardy indiscretion. Chelsea didn't think she could ever face her again.

Vaguely Chelsea wondered if Grace would tell her father. Even if she didn't, Chet was bound to hear Grace and Nick arguing; he was bound to ask questions. And where would that leave Nick? In the hot seat, to be sure. Resented. Distrusted. Just as she would be from this day on. Her life had turned into one unholy mess.

But of course the worst turn of events had been Katie's skipping off. The child could've been lost for days, could've died in a fall, and in Nick's opinion, it was all Chelsea's fault.

Chelsea leaned against one of the porch columns and shut her eyes tight. "Oh, Nick," she cried. Nothing would be hard to bear if only he'd said he loved her.

Chelsea finally pried herself away from the post and went down the walk to the mailbox. Night shadows veiled the yard, but returning to the house with the day's mail, she was still able to discern the strange orange markers lining the property boundaries.

"What the devil?" she whispered. She crossed the lawn and lowered herself to her haunches. Surveyor's markers!

During the day, Nick had had surveyors come by to mark off the property! The fluorescent stakes prodded at her through the dark like so many eviction notices.

She'd had enough. She wanted out. She marched into the house and straight to her office. She knew the information was in here somewhere. She turned the magazine rack upside down, scattering periodicals across the rug.

A few minutes later, she'd found it—the ad from the ski resort in the Adirondacks looking for a balloon pilot. She checked her watch. Was it too late to call? On the other hand, if she waited until morning, might she not lose her courage? She called.

When she hung up ten minutes later, she had an interview.

UNREAL. THAT WAS HOW the whole day felt. Chelsea barely remembered the long drive into New York or what she said during her seemingly endless interview. From the minute she'd decided to do this, her mind had shifted into numb. The fact that she actually landed the job only gave the day a deeper sense of unreality.

She wasn't sorry she'd made the move; she was just a little overwhelmed when she thought of everything that now had to be done. She had definitely dived in before thinking of the consequences.

The first step was a phone call to Larry, she decided, as she turned her Jeep into the driveway. If she was going to tie up all the loose ends of her life in three days, there wasn't a minute to waste.

Her van was parked in front of the barn, she noticed immediately. Nick had called her three times last night, but she hadn't picked up the phone. He'd finally left a message on her machine, saying he would be by in the morning to drop off her van. She'd left for New York before he'd arrived—

which was fine with her. She hoped she never saw Nick Tanner again.

"Larry? Hi. I can't talk long. I've got loads to do, but what I have to say is extremely important. So listen carefully. I've got a new job."

"What kind of job?" Larry sounded incredulous.

"I'm now vice president and chief pilot of Balloon the Adirondacks."

"You're *what?*"

"Remember that resort in upstate New York that was looking for someone to start up a hot-air balloon business? Well, I went for an interview today and got the job."

"I don't believe this!"

"Believe it, Lar. It's incredible—the job, the place!"

"Why?"

"Why not? Nick said I should be bolder when it came to business. So, I am."

"But why?"

Chelsea's contrived enthusiasm flagged. "I'm tired of fighting an uphill battle, and that's all my business has been. I'm throwing in the towel."

"After all those years of struggling? Oh, sis... Is the pay enough for you to live on?"

"Quite. In fact, I'd say it's pretty darn good."

"So, when do you start?"

"I said I'd be there in three days."

Larry choked in disbelief.

"That's why I'm calling. I still have two charters booked. Will you take them?"

"Sure. Yes, of course." He still sounded as if he'd been flattened by a steamroller.

"I'm also offering you the business. If you want it, Balloon the Berkshires is yours. Weekends, a few afternoons—that's all you really need to keep it going. It's never been more than a part-time venture, anyway. The only thing that was big-time was my imagination.''

Larry groaned as if too much was coming at him. ''What price are you asking?''

''Price? I don't want anything.''

''But you've established the name...''

''Zip. Nada. Please, Larry, take it. Keep it going.''

He must have heard the catch in her voice. ''Sure, sis. I have another question. Where are you gonna live?''

''In a condo. Slopeside,'' she answered, regaining her spark. ''The resort has overbuilt, and a lot of units are going begging. So...''

''Are you buying a condo?'' Larry asked, aghast.

''No, just renting. Really cheap, too. Hey, don't you want to hear about the job?''

''Oh, sure. Of course.''

''Well, this place is a full five-star, four-season resort. Not only is it a first-class ski area, it also has a golf course, a health club, four swimming pools and an ice-skating rink. Now they want to add hot-air balloon rides as a feature, and I'm the person who's going to head it up. I'll be in charge of the whole operation—hiring other pilots, buying equipment, scheduling, advertising.''

''It sounds like a lot of responsibility.''

''It is, but it's also the opportunity of a lifetime.''

''Is it really, sis? Is it worth it, moving and all?''

Chelsea fought against a wave of sadness. ''It sure is.''

''Well, if you're happy...''

''I am.''

''So, what about the house you're renting now?''

''Most of the furniture came with the place. It won't take me long to pack what's mine. A small rental truck and the van...''

''Mimi and I'll be over to help.''

"Thanks. I can use it. Larry, I have one more favor, and it's a big one."

"Fire away."

"The kids from the hospital..." Here her composure slipped. It was a moment before she went on. "I know I have no right foisting them on other people—I take them up free, and you'd be losing money. But do you suppose you could find the time to take on one or two? I'll ask a couple of other pilots if they'll share the rest. You don't have to do it indefinitely. Just cover the flights I've already promised, then you can dismantle the program." She waited, fingers crossed.

"Don't worry about the kids. I'll... do what I can."

"And make sure you include Katie Tanner."

"I won't forget Katie."

And neither will I, Chelsea thought, a tear sliding down her cheek.

CHAPTER THIRTEEN

NICK LOUNGED on a bench at the bottom of the slope and smiled as Katie came barreling down the alpine slide. Luckily, the slide hadn't officially opened yet, and no one was in danger of getting plowed over.

Nick cupped his hands around his mouth and hollered up the hill. "Hey, slow down. You're gonna jump the track."

She slowed—for about five seconds.

He slouched and rested his head on the top slat of the bench. The sky was milky blue and promised a warm, busy day at Pine Ridge. Nick's gaze roamed the blue dome, expecting to see Chelsea's balloon somewhere up there. Searching had become an automatic reflex.

Damn the woman! Damn! he swore, sitting up. He hadn't seen her in four days and hoped he never did again. He'd never known himself to lose his head so completely because of a woman. He'd forgotten his priorities, too, and Katie had suffered. But no more. He'd learned his lesson.

Not that there was any going back with Grace. They'd broken up, and he was glad finally to be free.

Katie braked to a shuddering stop on the level run of track at the base of the hill. "That was neat!" She laughed as she ran over, her leg noticeably stronger. "Can I go again?"

Nick checked his watch. "Once more."

"Neat. This is a lot better fun than last time."

"What last time?"

"With Grace." Katie's tongue lolled comically while she rolled her eyes.

"You really don't like her much, do you?"

"She yells at me. She don't let me even *move*."

A vague apprehension prickled along the back of Nick's neck. "The other day, before you went for your walk to the cave..." Katie inched away, and Nick imagined she was remembering the scolding he'd given her. "What did you and Grace do that afternoon, before your walk?"

"Nothin'. I wanted to go out. I wanted to ride my bike, but she had papers to typewrite. She made me watch TV."

A knot of anger twisted in Nick's chest. "How long?"

"All day. She didn't have time to watch me. She was very, very busy."

"I'll bet," Nick muttered.

"I'm sorry 'bout my walk. You got scared, huh?" Katie reached a hand to Nick's head and patted softly.

"Very scared, Spud."

"I won't do it again—unless you go with me. Will you, Dad?"

Nick looked hard into his daughter's eager blue eyes. "You had a pretty good time on your hike, didn't you?"

Her dimples deepened. "It was neat."

Nick groaned. The child had a streak of Chelsea in her as broad as the sky.

"Except for when I didn't know how to get down," she admitted, frowning.

"You know, there are lots of other places around here to hike. If you promise not to go off by yourself anymore..."

"I promise."

"Good. I know where there's a...a neat waterfall. Would you like to see that?"

She nodded, her eyes wide.

"We'll go Saturday. Now, you have time for one last slide."

Katie dragged her sled over to the chair lift where an obliging attendant let her hop another ride. Nick sat back watching her, but remembering the golden afternoon he'd spent with Chelsea at Bash Bish Falls. He missed her. He really missed her.

The beep of a car horn startled him. He turned. It was Chet Lockwood.

"Hey, Chet, what's up?" Nick walked toward the car.

"I was going to ask you the same thing. Did you know the Lawton girl got a job in New York?"

Nick felt as if he'd been sucker-punched. "Chelsea?"

Chet nodded indignantly. "She called me this morning to tell me she was leaving."

Nick reeled from another blow. "She's moving out of the house?"

"Moving? Why, she's gone. I've never seen anybody pack up and leave so fast. You had no idea, huh?"

Nick clutched the nape of his neck. "Uh...no. What did she say?"

"Not much. It's a very good job. A resort in the Adirondacks. She apologized for the rush, but they need her right away. That's about it."

Nick paced alongside the car. "She's gone?"

Chet snapped his fingers. "Just like that." He got out of his car and leaned against the fender. "Nick, you look like hell, you know that?"

Nick stopped his pacing and scanned his green polo shirt and worn jeans. "Thanks."

"Not the clothes. You. Not sleeping much these nights?"

Nick shrugged noncommittally.

"Mind if we talk? We haven't done much of that since you and Grace had your falling out."

Nick tensed. He hoped Chet wasn't about to urge a reconciliation.

"What I want to tell you is . . . well, I think it's okay that you two broke up. I thought you ought to know that."

Nick cocked his head warily. "I'm glad. I never meant to hurt her. Or you."

"I realize that. You're a man of integrity, Nick. I think you also ought to know that Grace is doing just fine. She sulked a day, then went right back to being her old self."

"Really?" This surprised Nick.

"I always had the feeling you two were forcing your romance. I never sensed any real spark."

Nick rested against the car beside the older man, chagrined.

"I think my daughter may be relieved it's over herself. For a while she was flattered you were taking her out, but she knows when something's not right. And I don't think she cares to settle for half measures."

"And she shouldn't. She deserves the fullest life possible."

"So do you, Nick."

Nick glanced away. He knew that longing for Chelsea clouded his eyes.

"It's about time you eased up on yourself and let it happen."

"What do you mean?"

"As I said before, you're a man of integrity, Nick. You judge yourself harder than anyone I know. It's why I enjoy having you as a partner. But give yourself a break. Listen to your heart. It's trying to tell you something."

"I don't think I understand."

"I think you do. I have the address of the resort she's moving to."

Nick felt an ache deep inside him, an ache that filled his heart and his head. "Am I that transparent?"

Chet laughed quietly. "Like glass. Why not give her a call?"

Nick chewed on the inside of his cheek. "What would be the point? She's made a decision, got a new job."

"The point is that you love her. Or haven't you figured that out yet?"

Nick's lungs filled, wouldn't release, and began to burn. "No! You're wrong." The vehemence of his answer startled them both.

"What are you afraid of, son?" Chet's broad face softened with compassion.

"Afraid? I'm not afraid." Even as he was speaking, Nick knew he was mouthing empty words. He'd always been wary of Chelsea. She reminded him of Laura, and Laura had been a mistake.

But she wasn't Laura, was she? Chelsea might make her living by unorthodox means, but she wasn't spoiled and reckless. She was the most caring person he'd ever met. And cautious. The only thing she had in common with Laura was that Nick found her exciting. No, it went beyond excitement. That was why he'd had her house lot surveyed and sectioned off from the rest of Pine Ridge. He'd decided to buy it, keep it separate from whatever happened to the ski area. He'd entertained daydreams of sharing the place with her. In unguarded moments he'd even envisioned the place alive with the laughter of children, their children....

Suddenly all the fight went out of him. He did love Chelsea, didn't he? She was the center of his universe, the fire in his veins. Why had it been so difficult for him to recognize that fact?

"Taking another chance is tough. Scary," Chet muttered softly, looking off into the hills. "Especially for someone like you who was so badly burned first time around. Laying yourself open to the possibility of being burned again is real tough. You think it's going to happen again. You think all kinds of awful things. That it won't last. That she'll be different from what you expect. You think she might go off and get herself . . ." Chet ducked his head. "Sorry, it's just that I hate to see you passing up the chance to be happy."

That was it. When all was said and done, Nick didn't really disapprove of Chelsea's livelihood or her influence on Katie. He was simply scared, scared of loving again.

But he did love her. He loved her more than his own life. The admission saddened him because it came too late. He loved her, and probably had from the moment he'd met her that blustery day in April, but he'd never had the courage to tell her, even when she'd admitted that she loved him.

He cringed. Chelsea had had a lot at stake, too, yet she'd gone out on that limb—only to find herself alone. What a jerk he was!

Chet's soft chuckle drew his attention. "You look about as down in the mouth as I've ever seen anyone. All isn't lost, you know."

"Could've fooled me."

"I can't believe you'll go after a business deal hammer and tongs, yet won't lift a finger to go after Chelsea."

"What am I supposed to do? I've given her nothing but grief. Why would she want to return?"

"Because *she* loves *you.*"

Nick watched Katie slide to a stop at the base of the hill again. "I should go."

"Well, it's been good talking to you."

"That it has."

"Uh, Nick?"

"Yes."

"Life isn't a tour of duty, you know."

Nick rapped his knuckles on the hood of the car and smiled ruefully. "Think you've got me pegged, huh?"

"I know I do." Chet slipped back into his car and flicked on the ignition. "Go after her, Nick. I'm sure a creative guy like you can find a way."

Nick smiled and waved Chet off. He hoped so, because he'd just discovered there was something more frightening than loving someone. It was having to live without the person you loved.

CHELSEA TURNED to view her backside in the full-length bathroom mirror. Her bathing suit still fit well enough, but it had definitely seen better days. Unfortunately, it was too late to do anything about that now. Her friends were meeting down at the pool in fifteen minutes.

She picked a towel off the rattan shelf and stuffed it into her carryall. Since taking this job a week ago, she'd made an effort to get to know her coworkers and enjoy all the facilities at her disposal; and of course she was thrilled to be living in so luxurious an apartment.

Hard as she tried to adjust, though, Chelsea knew the condo would never feel like home, and these people were not friends, just passing acquaintances.

It was ironic. She was finally making a good living at what she loved; she had a stylish condo, independence and security. Yet how she missed her life back home! The quirky old house, her tenuous charter business and of course her family. She called them frequently, but it wasn't the same as being able to drop by.

She missed them tremendously, but not half as much as she missed Nick. There wasn't an hour that went by that she didn't think about him or Katie and wish she could be with them again.

Still, she knew she'd done the right thing. She'd removed herself from the scene, leaving Nick and Grace to work things out without distraction.

Nick needed the room to sort out priorities. He'd been playing a game with her—and with himself—ever since their first meeting. He found her enticing, he liked giving in to the attraction occasionally and enjoying the electricity, but still he refused to give up whatever Grace provided him. He wanted to have his cake and eat it, too.

Well, damn him! He couldn't have it both ways! She was glad she'd packed up and left, she attested, swiping a tear from her cheek.

Her thoughts were shattered by the ring of the phone. She hurried from the bathroom, bare toes sinking into thick mauve carpet.

"Hello?"

"Chelsea?"

The world reeled and blurred. "Nick?" Was it really him? For a moment neither of them spoke.

"Yes," he finally answered. "How are you?"

She cleared her throat and attempted to sound collected. "Okay. Yourself?"

"I'm fine."

Chelsea let her knees follow their natural instinct and buckle. "And how's Katie?" she inquired, sinking into the soft cushions of the couch.

"Well, actually, she's the reason I'm calling."

Chelsea didn't like the edge in his voice. "Is anything the matter?"

"Afraid so."

"Has she had an accident? Is she sick?"

"No, nothing like that, but the situation's almost as serious." His words were growing cooler, edgier.

"What's the matter with her, Nick?"

"It's her therapy. I'm afraid she's regressing. I'll be damned if I can understand it." He sounded disgusted and tired, perhaps even a little angry.

Chelsea dropped her forehead to her palm and sighed, a shadow of guilt darkening her expression. "Hasn't Larry taken her up in his balloon?"

"No." The anger was becoming more pronounced. "He's busy, what with his regular job and other charters. It isn't easy to book time with him."

"Do you want me to speak to him?"

"No, don't bother. He isn't really the problem."

She gulped, another wave of guilt swamping her. "Oh? What is, then?"

"If you really want to know," he said crisply, "it's you, Chelsea. For some obscure reason, Katie wants no one but you to pilot her flights. She's being a first-rate brat about it, too."

"Oh, Nick. I hope you're not letting her get away with that. How are you handling it?"

He snorted contemptuously. "I'm not all that sure I ought to *handle* it. Naturally, I don't want her to act up, but I can understand why she's doing it. She feels betrayed and abandoned, and in all honesty I can see why."

"Nick!"

"Well, you did back out of your agreement, didn't you?"

"But... but I made provisions."

"You think a seven-year-old understands provisions?" His voice rasped with undisguised resentment now.

"Nick, what are you saying?"

"I'm saying I think you should fulfill your obligations."

"But how?"

"Don't you have any free time?"

Chelsea bristled under his cold sarcasm, her own attitude hardening. "Sure, I have free time. I'll meet you at my field Wednesday evening. Pardon me, *your* field—if it's still there, that is. For all I know you've already brought in your backhoes and cement mixers and dug it all up."

"The backhoes and cement mixers are there, but there's still room for your balloon."

"Good. Then I'll see you Wednesday."

"Good. And I'll be paying for this charter, too."

"I wouldn't consider any other terms." She hung up without even saying goodbye.

CHELSEA TRIED TO ACT blasé in front of Larry and Mimi, as if traveling a hundred and fifty miles to accommodate one little girl was as unimportant to her as sneezing. She told them she'd come home because she missed *them* and she was just fitting Katie in around the visit. She must have played her part well, she decided, because neither of them questioned her story.

The mask of cool, calm boredom could stretch just so far, however. Through afternoon chatter, through their early supper. By the time she reached the field, Chelsea's nerves were shot. She kept watching the road, waiting for a blue Volvo to appear. Her mouth got dryer, her palms sweatier.

"Here they come," Larry finally called out.

The sedan pulled off the road into the field and came to a stop by Chelsea's Jeep. She closed her eyes and whispered a prayer to get her through this moment.

Nick got out, looking better than her dreams had ever painted him. He was wearing a blue chambray shirt, sleeves rolled to the elbow, and soft faded jeans whose fit was practically indecent. In the two months she'd known him, he hadn't cut his hair, and now it curled with attractive abandon around his richly tanned face.

During the past couple of days, Chelsea had somehow convinced herself that she could see Nick and not be affected. How stupid could she be? Nick overwhelmed her. He took her breath away. Now she prayed just to get through the transaction with her dignity intact.

His gaze locked onto her almost immediately. She froze. After the stillest, most eternal moment she'd ever known, she forced herself to wave. "Hi, Nick."

He tossed a casual wave back and turned to talk to Larry. Chelsea expelled a long sigh.

Katie bounded over. Funny, but Chelsea couldn't see any evidence of the child's regressing. If anything, her leg seemed stronger. Chelsea gave her a huge hug. "Hi, kiddo.

Oooh, I've missed you." She had trouble keeping the tightness out of her voice. "And how did you do at therapy this week?"

"Good." Katie reached down into a pocket of her lavender sweatpants. "See, I got a ticket."

"Okay, then I owe you a ride."

"Are we almost ready?"

"We are ready already. Anytime you are, Spud."

Katie grinned. "Hey, that's what my Dad calls me." She looked back toward her father who was bent in quiet conversation with Larry and Mimi.

Chelsea fought down the hurt. Evidently he had no desire to speak to her at all. She didn't know why she should feel offended. Angry was what she should be. She'd come a hundred and fifty miles because he'd accused her of being irresponsible.

"I have to get my sweatshirt, Chelsea. I'll be right back."

"Sure enough." Chelsea turned and hoisted herself over the side of the basket. A moment later she heard the dull thump of someone landing behind her. She looked around, expecting to see Katie. When her gaze collided with Nick's, she gave out a small, alarmed cry.

"What are you doing here? You planning to join the flight?" She never got an answer. Nick was too busy untethering the balloon. Before she realized what he was doing, he tossed the cable to Larry and the basket began to lift.

"Oh, my Lord... Wait." Her eyes widened. "Wait, Larry. Katie's gone to the car for her sweatshirt."

Larry, however, seemed to have gone deaf. Faster than lightning, he and his wife moved away. They wouldn't even look at her.

"What's going on here?" Chelsea begged as the basket rose. She swiveled around to face Nick, panic in her eyes. "What's going on?" He seemed perfectly calm, hanging on to a guy wire with one hand.

Chelsea lunged for the cable connected to the deflation panel, only to have Nick's hand clamp around her wrist. She reached with her other hand, but was just as easily thwarted. No matter how many attempts she made, it was obvious she'd never get by Nick. Her shoulders sagged with defeat, and he let her go.

"You planned this! All of you!" she cried hoarsely as the balloon floated over the heads of her scheming relatives. "I've been tricked." When she glanced over the rail, Nick latched on to her arms again and pulled her to him.

"Let go! I'm not going to jump. How do you think *you'd* get down?" She broke free, even though the momentary contact with that solid chest had caused a soaring in her soul.

For a moment Chelsea thought she might cry. She was confused and hurt. It seemed everyone she knew had turned against her.

Larry's voice, fuzzy with static, leapt from the radio. "Hey, sis. How're things upstairs?"

In her anger, she considered not answering but finally reached for the receiver. "Fine, big brother. We've got a nice northeasterly breeze. Low humidity, good buoyancy..."

She suspected he picked up the frost in her reply. "Chelse, hey, don't be mad," he implored.

"I'll be whatever I want, thank you. Talk to you later." She snapped off their connection and slumped down onto one of the corner benches. As if in a daze she looked across and saw Nick confidently firing up the burner.

"What do you think you're doing?"

He winked. "Practicing. Since you went away, I've been taking lessons."

Chelsea's mouth dropped open.

As the balloon wafted higher into the sky, Nick looked down at her, that smoldering look she loved so much burning in his eyes. An unbidden excitement rippled along

Chelsea's spine. She was being kidnapped, by golly, shanghaied by a dark, sexy sky pirate. For one irrational moment she wanted to laugh out of pure glee, but she caught herself sharply. This wasn't in the least bit funny.

"Okay, Nick, let's cut the nonsense," she demanded. "What's going on?"

"I thought this would be the easiest way for us to talk. No interruptions, no place to run."

"And what about Katie. That story about her regressing..."

"I'm sorry, but I didn't think you'd come home just because I asked."

"All right." She sighed resignedly. "What do you want to talk about?"

"First of all, I'd like you to know that Chet Lockwood and I have discussed at great length the feasibility of having a hot-air balloon business running out of Pine Ridge. We both agree it'd be a terrific four-season attraction, and we'd like you to be the person heading up that business."

"What?" Chelsea whispered, stupefied.

"We'd like something similar to the operation you're involved in now. We'll guarantee you the same pay and whatever benefits they're offering."

Chelsea shot to her feet. "I don't believe your gall! What do you think I am, Nick Tanner? Some kind of puppet who can be yanked one way and then another? Why didn't you say something before I accepted this other job and went through all the trouble of uprooting myself?"

"I don't know," he admitted in frustration, "and for that, all I can say is, I'm sorry. I *thought* about it a lot. I just didn't realize you'd put me on a clock and my time was running out."

The balloon had leveled off and was drifting softly toward the gray-green slopes of Pine Ridge Mountain. A glance over the instruments and down to the road told

Chelsea that everything was under control. She returned her attention to this man, this infuriatingly wonderful man, whose musky scent alone could rob her of any powers of logic.

"We've discussed other ideas, too," he went on, "like the bed-and-breakfast tour I once mentioned, and we've looked into hosting rallies. I realize you might not have the time or inclination to get involved with so much activity. The scope of this thing would be your decision entirely."

Chelsea placed a hand to her head. She had to think, had to retrieve her perspective. She supposed she could quit her new job without causing a major upset. She'd only been at it for two weeks, hardly long enough to become indispensable. Besides, one of the other pilots she'd hired had a family and needed the job more than she did. He wasn't quite as experienced, but she had no doubt he'd do fine. Still...

"I...I don't have any place to live."

"The house you used to rent's available."

"Sure, but for how long?" she asked sarcastically.

"Indefinitely. It's been portioned off from Pine Ridge and sold. It's a separate property now."

"Sold? To whom?"

"Me."

Chelsea laughed incredulously. "I'd be renting from you personally? Terrific."

"If you want the place, I'm sure we can negotiate mutually agreeable terms."

Her powers of reasoning were getting fuzzier. Move back? Enter into business with Chet Lockwood? How could she do that after what she'd done to his daughter? "Are you sure Chet is in full agreement?"

"He's crazy about the idea. Why wouldn't he be?"

"Well..." Her cheeks warmed. "I thought Grace might've mentioned..."

A smile of compassion flicked through his expression. "It's over, Chelse. Grace is gone from my life. She never should've been there in the first place."

Chelsea clutched her hands to control their trembling. "Does *she* know it's over?"

His smile broadened. "Yes. We talked the whole thing out."

"And Chet doesn't hold any grudges?"

Nick shook his head, his eyes trained on her. "Neither does Grace. They'd both feel privileged to have you aboard. So would I."

Chelsea felt her defenses crumbling. With those last few words, she wanted nothing more than to fall into Nick's arms. She had to remind herself that he was only offering her a job, not his love.

She glanced away, over the endless green hills and lakes touched by the gold of the lowering sun. "I don't know, Nick. I'll have to think about it."

He moved a few steps toward her, closing the distance that separated them. Her thoughts scrambled. Being here felt unreal. She looked at the sky and the hills and now at Nick's ruggedly handsome face as if through a haze. It was so blessedly wonderful to be with him again that the joy was almost too much to bear.

Was he really reaching out to her, she wondered groggily, or was she only dreaming it? When his fingers touched her cheek, she still wasn't sure. She only knew that her heart was fluttering at an unholy rate and her body felt as if it could float without the balloon.

"Chelsea, I had to talk to you for another reason. It wasn't just to offer you a job." His thumb stroked the line of her jaw. A mesmerizing glint intensified his stare. "We have to straighten out this misunderstanding between us. Larry told me you moved away because of the opportunity this new job offered you, but I can't help thinking it had a lot more to do with what happened in my apartment."

"D-did something happen?"

"It certainly did. We were having a conversation, of sorts. I believe you were in the process of telling me you loved me."

Chelsea thought she would die of mortification right there and then. "I'm sorry. It was a ridiculous thing to say. I shouldn't have."

"Especially since I didn't return the sentiment?"

Chelsea turned away, but there was no place she could go. He turned her to face him again.

"I thought perhaps if I got you alone we could continue that conversation." He pulled her against him, and she pressed her face into his shirtfront, wanting to cry for reasons she couldn't fathom anymore.

"I wasn't looking for a response, Nick. I realize I'm not the sort of person you care to take seriously. You know what you want, and I simply fall short of the mark. It's no big deal."

He folded her closer, his body molding itself to hers. "Don't say that. Don't even think it. *I* was the one who was all messed up, and for what it's worth, I'm sorry I didn't answer you that day. My body was trying to tell you what was in my heart, but I realize now some things should be spelled out more clearly."

Chelsea pulled back to put a little space between them so that she could look up into his face. She couldn't quite figure out that boyish expectancy in his voice. It was then that she realized the balloon was drifting directly above Pine Ridge, and as if a voice were calling to her, she looked down toward the ski area.

Through the trees, she could see a sign draped across the sloping roof of the chalet that housed Nick's office. "Chelsea, I love you," it read for all the world to see. And on the far broader roof of the main dining hall stretched another. "Chelsea, I love you," it also read.

Chelsea clasped her hands to her mouth as she drew in a sob. "Oh, Nick, did you do that? All the trouble..."

"It was," he agreed dryly. "I used every sheet I owned."

She laughed on a hiccup. "That's just about the most romantic gesture I've ever heard of."

"You were overdue. Our courtship hasn't exactly been the most idyllic affair so far. I've kicked and bucked it most of the way. But you ought to know I can be a very romantic guy. In fact, from now on, you're going to think you've hooked up with the king of romance." Nick smiled lovingly at her. "I've missed you, Chelse," he whispered, touching his forehead to hers.

"I've missed you, too."

He tilted her chin and pressed her lips softly with his own. His breath shuddered as he drew away. She wrapped her arms around his shoulders and pulled him closer. When their lips met again, all their longing, all their love and desire, came together.

"I love you, Chelse. I can't imagine my life without you in it." He stroked back her hair, wiped the wetness from her cheek.

Chelsea would have said something then, but another rooftop sign was caught in her peripheral vision. She turned slightly, just as Nick whispered, "Marry me," repeating the message peeking up through the trees. "Marry me, please."

Was this really happening, Chelsea wondered, or was she caught within some sorcerer's dream? She looked into Nick's eyes and knew she wasn't dreaming. They were really at the beginning of a new life together.

She nodded. "Yes, of course I'll marry you."

"Soon."

All she was able to do was nod before he captured her in another kiss. Through the fog clouding her mind, she remembered to reach up and fire the burner to give them a safer drifting altitude. Then she returned her full attention to the kiss that was deepening and turning her bones to water. Apparently it was having a similar effect on Nick, because she soon discovered that they were lying on the floor of the basket.

The radio crackled into life. "Some surprise, huh, Chelse?" Her brother laughed. "We were up doing those signs till almost one in the morning. I was beat today, let me tell you."

Katie giggled. "Hi, Dad. Hi, Chelsea."

Then Mimi rattled on about how hard it had been to keep the secret and how she was afraid Katie wouldn't be able to.

Chelsea felt Nick's mouth curve into a smile. Their breath mingled in a shared laugh.

"They don't have to come along on our honeymoon, do they?" Nick asked.

"I'll see what I can work out."

"Mmm. You do that," he murmured as his lips worked their slow way down her neck.

"Hey, can you guys hear us?" Mimi questioned. "Larry, do you think something's wrong with the radio?"

Chelsea knew she'd have to answer them sooner or later. She also knew the balloon would eventually have to land. But not yet. Just for a while longer, she and Nick would sail on through the silent dusk. And though she knew in body she'd soon be back, her heart would never come down to earth again.

"GET AWAY FROM IT ALL" SWEEPSTAKES

HERE'S HOW THE SWEEPSTAKES WORKS

NO PURCHASE NECESSARY

To enter each drawing, complete the appropriate Official Entry Form or a 3" by 5" index card by hand-printing your name, address and phone number and the trip destination that the entry is being submitted for (i.e., Caneel Bay, Canyon Ranch or London and the English Countryside) and mailing it to: Get Away From It All Sweepstakes, P.O. Box 1397, Buffalo, New York 14269-1397.

No responsibility is assumed for lost, late or misdirected mail. Entries must be sent separately with first class postage affixed, and be received by: 4/15/92 for the Caneel Bay Vacation Drawing, 5/15/92 for the Canyon Ranch Vacation Drawing and 6/15/92 for the London and the English Countryside Vacation Drawing. Sweepstakes is open to residents of the U.S. (except Puerto Rico) and Canada, 21 years of age or older as of 5/31/92.

For complete rules send a self-addressed, stamped (WA residents need not affix return postage) envelope to: Get Away From It All Sweepstakes, P.O. Box 4892, Blair, NE 68009.

© 1992 HARLEQUIN ENTERPRISES LTD.   SWP-RLS

"GET AWAY FROM IT ALL" SWEEPSTAKES

HERE'S HOW THE SWEEPSTAKES WORKS

NO PURCHASE NECESSARY

To enter each drawing, complete the appropriate Official Entry Form or a 3" by 5" index card by hand-printing your name, address and phone number and the trip destination that the entry is being submitted for (i.e., Caneel Bay, Canyon Ranch or London and the English Countryside) and mailing it to: Get Away From It All Sweepstakes, P.O. Box 1397, Buffalo, New York 14269-1397.

No responsibility is assumed for lost, late or misdirected mail. Entries must be sent separately with first class postage affixed, and be received by: 4/15/92 for the Caneel Bay Vacation Drawing, 5/15/92 for the Canyon Ranch Vacation Drawing and 6/15/92 for the London and the English Countryside Vacation Drawing. Sweepstakes is open to residents of the U.S. (except Puerto Rico) and Canada, 21 years of age or older as of 5/31/92.

For complete rules send a self-addressed, stamped (WA residents need not affix return postage) envelope to: Get Away From It All Sweepstakes, P.O. Box 4892, Blair, NE 68009.

© 1992 HARLEQUIN ENTERPRISES LTD.   SWP-RLS

"GET AWAY FROM IT ALL"

Brand-new Subscribers-Only Sweepstakes

OFFICIAL ENTRY FORM

This entry must be received by: May 15, 1992
This month's winner will be notified by: May 31, 1992
Trip must be taken between: June 30, 1992—June 30, 1993

YES, I want to win the Canyon Ranch vacation for two. I understand the prize includes round-trip airfare and the two additional prizes revealed in the BONUS PRIZES insert.

Name _____

Address _____

City _____

State/Prov._____ Zip/Postal Code_____

Daytime phone number _____
                          (Area Code)

Return entries with invoice in envelope provided. Each book in this shipment has two entry coupons — and the more coupons you enter, the better your chances of winning!
© 1992 HARLEQUIN ENTERPRISES LTD.   2M-CPN

"GET AWAY FROM IT ALL"

Brand-new Subscribers-Only Sweepstakes

OFFICIAL ENTRY FORM

This entry must be received by: May 15, 1992
This month's winner will be notified by: May 31, 1992
Trip must be taken between: June 30, 1992—June 30, 1993

YES, I want to win the Canyon Ranch vacation for two. I understand the prize includes round-trip airfare and the two additional prizes revealed in the BONUS PRIZES insert.

Name _____

Address _____

City _____

State/Prov._____ Zip/Postal Code_____

Daytime phone number _____
                          (Area Code)

Return entries with invoice in envelope provided. Each book in this shipment has two entry coupons — and the more coupons you enter, the better your chances of winning!
© 1992 HARLEQUIN ENTERPRISES LTD.   2M-CPN